Ditchmen 3

THE RISE OF DIRT CAKE

Joe Ginter

ISBN 979-8-88644-070-6 (Paperback)
ISBN 979-8-88644-071-3 (Digital)

Covenant Books
11661 Hwy 707
Murrells Inlet, SC 29576
www.covenantbooks.com

To Mom
There are no struggles now, just enjoying.

Acknowledgments

To my fifth-grade language arts students of the 2021–2022 school year, who were my test audience, my proofreaders, my advisors, and my promoters. Your efforts in the filming of the commercial for *Ditchmen 2* were so motivating in catapulting our efforts to complete *Ditchmen 3: The Rise of Dirt Cake*.

I hope you will always remember how we found the courage to "enjoy the struggle" and create the new direction in the Ditchmen story. To my past language arts students involved in the Ditchmen trilogy, continued thanks for keeping the dream going. As requested, here is an improved terminology key:

- Fade in: a process in which the picture is from a darkened screen to a fully lighted screen.
- Fade out: the same process as above in reverse.
- Cut to: an editing technique that generally is avoided and left normally to the director to determine abrupt camera transitions. It is used in this book to help the reader with what they visualize next.
- Dissolve to: used as a time lapse, not to be confused with cutting from shot to shot.
- Series of shots: literally a series of shots run one after another.
- Close-up: a shot that emphasizes a detail, for example, a ball or a sign.
- Close shot: shows a character from the shoulders up.
- POV shot: abbreviation for point of view. It is a cinematic trick used to present a scene so the audience sees it through the eyes of a particular character.

- Pan shot: a horizontal camera movement in which the camera pivots left or right while its base remains in a fixed location.

FADE IN

OFF SCREEN the opening song begins, "My Town" by the Michael Stanley Band. Superimposed on screen is Ditchmen 3: The Rise of Dirt Cake, *as well as opening credits.*

SERIES OF SHOTS this beautiful, sunny late October Saturday morning of the various landmarks from the first two screenplays of the St. Marys, Ohio, area. This includes windmills with a nearby farmer in his combine harvester, Griner's Farm, the rural cemetery, and the country road adjacent to Griner's Farm and the cemetery. The country road has been completely resurfaced and the bunker underneath filled in. Other shots include Ted's rural home, the present-day cemetery in town, Amy's new lab completely funded by the government catty-corner from the cemetery, the school, and the restored theater downtown and also not previously mentioned locations and items like the town's historic canal boat and museum, "Reelect Ted Horn for Mayor" signs, banners promoting Halloween Week, and a sign promoting the annual Ghost Ball and, finally, a new wellness-and-fitness center decorated with grand opening banners and posters promoting its open house event.

Song ends.

CUT TO

Ted Horn walking out of his rural country home with real estate client, Vance Wringer, right behind him. Ted is attempting to sell this property. Vance is a recently retired professional bodybuilder but nowhere the success and notoriety of an Arnold Schwarzenegger. He seems very personable, and his age would be approximately between Jay and Clay. They are facing the country road.

TED HORN. Gotta love the peace and quiet you get out here.

Vance Wringer. Very nice.

Ted Horn. There is said to be some fascinating history to this property.

Vance Wringer, *interrupting*. This is one of the places that frontiersman Simon Girty slid into the depths of inhumanity by massacring and pillaging a bunch of settlers. Their remains are probably still buried here.

Ted Horn. That's right. Very impressive. I'm only selling it because my wife, Leslie, and I are downsizing from three properties.

CUT TO

MEDIUM SHOT of a tall wooden fence built near the Ditchmen to provide protection from the Ditchmen when they existed.

CUT TO

Vance Wringer. Why the fence? To keep out Ditchmen?

Ted Horn. So you know about the Ditchmen? Of course, you do. Who doesn't? Yes, I put that fence there for protection. But it's not needed anymore. The bunker under the road has been completely filled in. Things are back to normal here.

Vance Wringer. What ever happened to Amy Griner and her research?

Ted Horn. The government built her a real-nice state-of-the-art lab in town. Haven't heard anything lately about her research. We're an exciting, growing community. That lab and your new fitness-and-wellness center help make my administration look successful.

Vance Wringer. I see. Are you coming to my grand opening slash open house?

Ted Horn. But of course, I wouldn't miss it especially since I'm the mayor. How exciting, former professional bodybuilder, Vance Wringer, moving to our community and opening up the Have a Fit, Stay Fit Wellness Center.

Vance Wringer. And you're a mayor who I understand is in the middle of a reelection campaign.

Ted Horn. That's correct. I'm being opposed by former-mayor Woody Burns. He doesn't play nicely with others.

Vance Wringer. Well then, I will make a contribution to your campaign immediately after I write you a check for this property.

Ted Horn. Gee, thanks! Wait, a check, no financing? I have a sale!

Vance Wringer. You have a sale. It's perfect for my purposes.

Ted Horn. That's wonderful. You'll love it here.

Vance Wringer. I believe I will.

Ted Horn. How exactly did you come to choose our town?

Vance Wringer. I've been itching to settle down and enjoy the quiet life. To be honest, the publicity of Ditchmen is what inadvertently educated me about your community. I always wanted to live in a place that has lots of traditions. It would be like being in a *Hallmark* movie. Just look in the last three months. You've had a "Back in the Day Days" Festival, a Homecoming Week, and now a Halloween Week culminating in a Ghost Ball. That sounds wild.

Ted Horn. It is, with everybody dressed as ghosts. You can't tell who's who. We have compiled quite an extensive calendar of events. I guess that's another accomplishment of my administration.

Vance Wringer. Plus, I love that sign as you come into town, "where living is a pleasure." How quickly can I move in?

Ted Horn. Immediately!

Vance Wringer. Excellent!

They enter back into the house, and the camera PANS *over to the country road as Jay and Amy Griner drive by in their vehicle heading toward town.*

OFF SCREEN *you hear the guitar interlude in the middle of the rock song "Crazy" by the John Hall Band.*

CUT TO

CLOSE SHOT *of Jay and Amy in their vehicle as he sings the last verse.*

JAY, *singing*. When you hold me, keep me up all night. You make it easy to forget about the trouble that we see. Should anybody love somebody this much. That this madness is magic to me. It's crazy. It feels like it will never end. And it's stronger, stronger than it's ever been. As the years go by, it will lift us higher, and there's no (Amy, no) way (Amy, way) to ever put out the fire. And I keep on falling, keep on falling in love. Falling back again, I keep on falling, keep on falling in love. And I keep on falling, keep on falling, keep on falling, keep on falling. And I keep on falling, keep on falling in love.

AMY, *sarcastically*. Wonderful, honey.

JAY. That was the John Hall Band. He was in the band, Orleans. They sang "Still the One." He went on to be a congressman. Come on, honey. Snap out of it. It's a beautiful Saturday morning.

AMY. Thank you, Cliff Clavin or Paul Blart? (*pause*) It's been fourteen months since Clay put you-know-what right in my hands, and I have made no headway.

JAY. Quit putting so much pressure on yourself. The you-know-what caused you to go in a completely different direction. There was bound to be some roadblocks.

AMY. But people are expecting some pretty big things from my research.

JAY. You got to quit wanting it so much and just let the science happen. At least, that's what you would tell me.

AMY. That's exactly what I would tell you. And you would tell me to enjoy the struggle.

JAY. So tell yourself that. You don't need me saying it.

Jay then begins to bellow out an old familiar melody.

JAY. To the dump, to the dump, to the dump, dump, dump.

AMY. How did a popular diner get the nickname the Dump?

JAY. Well, it's called Happy Humpty. There's a big revolving lighted sign of Humpty Dumpty sitting on a wall. I imagine Dump is short for Dumpty.

AMY. I should have figured that out a long time ago.

JAY. You were too busy thinking about the Big Guy Burger or the Ham Dandy.

AMY. Actually, I'm thinking about the Top of the Morning Breakfast Special. It was between this and the Moderate Breakfast or the Hearty Breakfast Special.

CUT TO

Inside the local diner as it is serving Saturday-morning breakfast to their customers.

CUT TO

A wall decoration promoting the diner's Ditchmen French toast sticks.

CUT TO

Retired Sheriff Al, Retired Police Chief Tim, and still current High School Principal Greg with their wives at a big table.

CUT TO

Jay and Amy entering the diner. Although it's not exactly like Norm entering the bar on the television show Cheers, *they receive a warm reception. Jay and Amy make their way to the table of the three other couples who were just mentioned who already got their drinks.*

WAITRESS. How are you guys this morning?

JAY AND AMY. We're good. Fine.

WAITRESS. What will it be this morning? Uh-oh, you're not.

JAY. Yes, it's that good of a morning, so a round of toast for the entire diner!

The diner customers cheer with exaggeration as if they just won the lottery.

JAY. And Ditchmen French toast sticks for me.

AMY. The Top of the Morning Breakfast Special for me, thanks.

JAY. You know why I do that?

AMY. I wouldn't be surprised why.

JAY. I'm instilling my new positive saying. Be like toast.

AMY. Be like toast?

JAY. Yes, even when you get burnt, you still pop up.

RETIRED SHERIFF AL. Are you guys going to the open house?

JAY. For the Have a Fit, Stay Fit Wellness Center? I believe we are.

AMY. Might as well. I'm at an impasse at the lab.

RETIRED POLICE CHIEF TIM, *across the table.* Have you met the owner, Vance Wringer, yet?

TIM'S WIFE. He seems awful nice. And with Tim retired, it makes sense for us to join.

PRINCIPAL GREG. You know, Jay, we never gave these two a retirement party.

AL. What are you talking about? We each had one.

JAY. I believe those were receptions. Greg's right. We need to take the two of you out tonight and relive something from our youth. The prefix *re* means a backward recall.

TIM. I'm sure Al would agree that this idea scares us to death.

CUT TO

MEDIUM SHOT of Jay and Amy beginning a brief quiet private chat.

JAY. We'll have to stop back home before the open house.

AMY. Why? What's up?

JAY. I forgot to bring an extra ostomy bag.

AMY. You can't go a few hours without having an extra bag?

JAY. You know I'm paranoid without having an extra bag just in case of a leak.

AMY. So be like all the toast that you just ordered, and pop up if you get burnt.

JAY. Okay, I'll give it a go, and hope it doesn't go the wrong way.

AMY. I'm proud of you.

In case you have forgotten, Jay was suffering from Crohn's disease when his large intestine perforated and it had to be removed along with three feet of his small intestine at the age of twenty-one. An emergency operation left him in need of an ileostomy bag in order to perform a number

*two. An ileostomy bag located in his lower abdomen can on occasion leak
and create a very embarrassing hit-the-fan situation for him.*

CUT TO
SERIES OF SHOTS *all the waitresses deliver plates of toast to the entire diner
as Jay receives lots of "thank-yous."*

DISSOLVE TO
LONG SHOT *of the outside of the Have a Fit, Stay Fit Wellness Center.*

CUT TO
SERIES OF SHOTS *of the inside of this new facility including the various
fitness rooms including cardio and strength machines, free weights, and
CrossFit and also the pool, walking track, massage rooms, cozy lounge
areas, and something called The Dirt Cake Dessert Bar.*

CUT TO
Al and Tim checking out one of the fitness rooms.
INTO FRAME *Vance arrives and greets them.*

VANCE. You know it's 25 percent off membership for first responders
and veterans.

TIM. But we're retired.
VANCE. Once a first responder, always a first responder.
TIM. Gee, we appreciate that.
AL. Yes, thank you.
VANCE. No, thank you.

CUT TO
Debbie, who has postponed finishing college to be one of the managers, is showing Clay one of the other fitness rooms.

CLAY. This place is incredible.
DEBBIE. Didn't I tell you?
CLAY. The capital to do something like this had to be enormous.
DEBBIE, *wearing her work uniform.* I wouldn't have postponed my college education to become a manager if I didn't think it'd be worthwhile.

INTO FRAME Vance once again.

VANCE. Hello, Debbie, this must be Clay.
DEBBIE. Clay, this is my boss and the owner, Mr. Wringer.
CLAY. Nice to meet you, sir. Quite an impressive place.
VANCE. Call me Vance. Glad you like it. Debbie tells me that you work for Amy Griner in her new lab. Now, that's what I call impressive.
CLAY. Yes, I guess. Gee, thanks.
VANCE. No, thank you. Do you know if she is coming here today?
CLAY. I think so.
VANCE. Great. I would love to meet her. I'm a big fan of her work. Debbie, make sure he tries the dirt cake. I gotta keep moving. (*EXITS FRAME.*)
CLAY. Dirt cake?
DEBBIE. It's this incredible healthy dessert that he is so proud of. It's an old family recipe.
CLAY. So you actually talk about me to your boss?

DEBBIE. Of course, I do. He's a great guy who cares about the interest of his employees.
CLAY. I'm your interest? That's great!
DEBBIE, *laughing*. You know you're a dirt cake!

CUT TO
Ted and Leslie Horn sitting in a cozy lounge area enjoying a healthy coffee and a bowl of dirt cake.

LESLIE. This dirt cake is delicious.
TED, *looking at his coffee*. What makes this a healthy coffee?
LESLIE. Let's see, it's organic, caffeine-free, low sugar, fat-free creamer, cinnamon and cocoa added.
TED. Is that all?

INTO FRAME is Ted's opponent in the upcoming mayor election, Woody Burns. He is short, bald, older, and extremely obnoxious. Woody is sort of a combination of Hollywood villain Sydney Greenstreet and Boss Hogg of the Dukes of Hazards.

WOODY BURNS. Well, well, well, if it isn't my worthy opponent. Are you taking a break from preparing for next Saturday's debate?
LESLIE, *to Ted*. Now's a good time. Go ahead.
TED. Yes, Woody, I am taking a break. Say, I have been meaning to ask you. Why did we schedule a debate the same night of the annual Ghost Ball? Let's change the day.
WOODY. No, no, no, I don't think so. The debate date stays the same.
LESLIE. Come on. Be reasonable.
WOODY. I wish I could, but believe me. I can't.
LESLIE. What's unbelievable is you at a fitness center.

INTO FRAME arrive Jay and Amy.

AMY. Hey, Leslie, Ted, good to see you. (*She doesn't even notice Woody Burns standing nearby.*)
LESLIE. Amy, you got to try this dirt cake.

TED. And the coffee. It's healthy.

WOODY. By all means, join your friends here. Linking you to them is exactly my best campaign strategy.

JAY. What is Boss Hogg talking about?

WOODY. Nothing, nothing at all. I'm sure this community is fine with its mayor associating with the local Dr. Mrs. Frankenstein.

JAY. Where's the medicine balls? I want to play dodgeball with Woody.

INTO FRAME Vance once again conducting his host duties.

VANCE. How's everybody here?

WOODY. Fabulous, your open house here is icing the election. It gives more evidence of the association between the mayor of our fair community and the person who attacked our fair community.

AMY. Sorry, Ted.

TED. No need. I'm not worried.

LESLIE. That's my man.

VANCE. Their friendship is why I became one of his biggest donors. I'm a fan. (*Reaches out to introduce himself to Amy.*) Vance Wringer.

AMY. Nice to meet you. My husband, Jay.

VANCE, *to Woody.* You can now go over to the membership table.

WOODY, *to Ted.* I will see you Saturday unless you decide to go hide at the Ghost Ball. (*Then to Vance.*) I don't need the membership. I need the latrine. You do have one in this monstrosity?

VANCE. That door over there on your right.

WOODY. Thank you, good day.

JAY. I still say where's your medicine balls. We'll pretend Woody is a dirt chick.

Everyone chuckles.

VANCE. No need. That's not the door to the bathroom. It's the door to the youth dodgeball league demonstration.

CUT TO

Woody inside the gym where the youth dodgeball demonstration is taking place. He is being bombarded from all sides as he makes a futile attempt to duck and swerve the oncoming balls like a teen from the 1960s doing the Watusi dance. OFF SCREEN briefly is the song "Wah Watusi" by the Orlons.

CUT TO

VANCE, *to Amy.* I was just talking about you to an employee of yours.

AMY. Has to be Clay since he's our only employee. And as a fan, you got to be disappointed in me. I'm in a bit of a rut with my research.

VANCE. Isn't that the life of a scientist?

JAY. That's what I tell her.

VANCE. Sometime, I would love a quick tour of your new lab.

AMY. Anytime. Debbie, who works for you, knows how to reach us.

VANCE. That's great. Thank you.

OFF SCREEN they hear somebody at the dirt cake bar yell, "This is fabulous!"

CUT TO

Coach sitting at the dirt cake bar having a wonderful introduction to dirt cake.

CUT TO

JAY. Do you serve potato chips? Coach loves potato chips.

VANCE. Potato chips? Excuse me, I don't want to miss an opportunity to receive praise for my dirt cake.

Vance EXITS FRAME.

AMY. He seems like a great guy.
LESLIE. I agree.
TED. I am glad you think so. He's your new neighbor.
JAY. You sold him your country property?

CUT TO
Coach still wolfing down dirt cake.

INTO FRAME arrives Vance.

VANCE. So you like my dirt cake?
COACH. Like it? Love it!
VANCE. You must like Oreo cookies then.
COACH. Yes, I do. Only I don't twist. I eat the chocolate wafers outside first and save the cream filling on my finger to eat last.
VANCE. Wow, that's the opposite from most. By the way, Coach, my facility is available for free anytime you want to hold a training session for your players.
COACH. Wow, really, that would be really super! Thank you!
VANCE. No, thank you!

DISSOLVE TO
Inside the new lab as Amy, Jay, and Clay walk in. Just like the Have a Fit, Stay Fit Wellness Center, everything is brand-new.

CLAY. Boy, Vance Wringer is sure a great guy.
JAY. Why does that sound like you are being sarcastic? Are you being an insecure goober?
AMY. You do sound suspicious. So he's a great guy. He's too old for Debbie and too young for me. You're both safe.

JAY. Good to know. You see, Clay, there's a lot of opportunities to be an insecure goober when your wife is so admired like mine.

AMY. Aw, that's so sweet.

CLAY. I'm not being an insecure goober here. It's just that no one is that doggone nice. And how can someone build such an elaborate place right here? We're not a huge market, and he didn't exactly have an Arnold Schwarzenegger-like career. There's something fishy about him.

JAY, *to Amy*. So what exactly are you going to show your new admirer when he comes over for a tour? Are you actually going to show him what Clay and Debbie found in one of the Ditchmen remains?

AMY. That was dumb of me. I can't explain the new direction of my research yet. I don't dare show the temporal lobe.

CUT TO
CLOSE-UP of a temporal lobe that was in the head of one of the Ditchmen. It is meticulously displayed in a large case like it was a Babe Ruth-autographed baseball. The case is mounted on an elaborate rotisserie filled with dirt. This contraption has two separate compartments holding canisters that dirt slowly trickles into once it leaves the rotisserie.

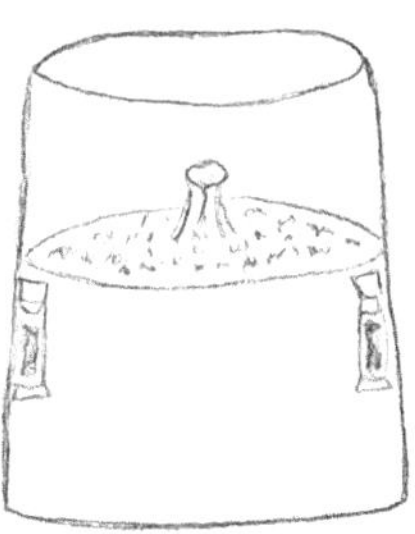

JAY. (*OFF SCREEN.*) There it is, the temporal lobe, placed right in your hands by Debbie and Clay, and we treated it like a sack lunch.

CUT TO
MEDIUM SHOT of the three still in the lab.

CLAY. I thought it was just a piece of steak when I first found it. Then I remembered that Ditchmen don't eat anything let alone a filet mignon.

AMY. The temporal lobe is vital to processing sensory input including pain and auditory stimuli. It helps us understand language, retain vision memories, and, most interesting, process and remember emotion.

JAY. You sound like you're rehearsing your tour.

CLAY. I, myself, needed the review.

AMY. It doesn't dare be part of the tour. It proved that the Ditchmen were developing. I am no longer entirely focusing a cure for cancer or paralysis. Woody Burns was right. I am Dr. Mrs. Frankenstein.

JAY. So you're not going to clue him in on how you are actually separating positive contaminated dirt and negative contaminated dirt.

CLAY. And remind me how does dirt get this positive or negative contamination?

AMY. From the aura in the dirt under the graves that we're bringing in from across the street or more like catty-corner. Then these aura remnants from the souls under the graves somehow get manifested from the windmills' by-product and the agriculture runoff that accumulate in the ditches. The temporal lobe then acts as magnet separating the positive ions from the negative.

CLAY. So it's like one of those Wooly Willy toys only instead of metal fillings, it is actual dirt.

JAY. Dear, you're not Dr. Mrs. Frankenstein. You are more like Dr. Jekyll and Mrs. Hyde. Uh-oh, our excavation project.

AMY. Right, you got to clean up the dirt tracks in here. This place has got to be spic-and-span.

CLAY. Spic-and-span?

Jay walks over to the back door and looks out.

JAY. Won't he just think it came from the grader out back here doing the final landscape for the building?

CLAY. He'll never suspect we are getting that dirt from a new tunnel and bunker from the cemetery.

JAY. New and improved tunnel and bunker.

AMY. Are we just starting this Ditchmen terror stuff all over again?

JAY. No, we're not. Just as long as you find a proper way to dispose of that negative dirt.

AMY, *holding up two canisters that were connected to the display.* It's a slow process. All I got is one canister of each.

JAY. Come on, Clay. Let's grab a couple of mops and get started. We both got things to do tonight.

DISSOLVE TO

Clay in the 1973 blue Chevy Nova that he bought from Jay. He hasn't quite had the chance to restore it yet. He pulls into the dark parking lot of the new fitness/wellness center to pick up Debbie. She comes out, and as she starts to put her backpack in the backseat, she notices once again that there is no floorboard.

DEBBIE. I keep forgetting there's no floorboard back here. I can't believe you bought this from Jay.

CLAY. What? It's a 1973 Chevy Nova. It was his car in high school. I will eventually get it completely restored.

DEBBIE. Man, what a day. I am so tired and yet so wired.

CLAY. Successful open house I take it.

DEBBIE. Amazing open house. Vance is going to knock it out of the ballpark with this place. We had tons of membership applications.

CLAY. You want to eat or catch a movie?

DEBBIE. Just a movie where I can just chill out would be great.

CLAY. You got it.

DEBBIE. I do appreciate how supportive you've been in all this. No hassle about taking a break from college. No insecure comments about my boss, Vance.

CLAY. You mean no insecure goober?

DEBBIE. Goober?

CLAY, *knowing he's not sincere.* Never mind, I'm just here to support.

Debbie gives him a peck on the cheek as he prepares to park.

DISSOLVE TO
LONG SHOT of Amy's lab with a view of the present-day cemetery in the background.

CUT TO
Amy working at her lab. She turns on her Alexa device.

OFF SCREEN the song "Monster Mash" by Bobby Pickett begins to play.

She sings along with some subtle dance moves near the temporal lobe display case as she retrieves the canister that contains the positive tainted dirt. She walks it over to an elevator and goes to the basement. Once in the basement, which is very new and clean except for a giant tarp that is fastened against the wall, Amy lifts the tarp and enters the recently constructed tunnel that leads to a bunker underneath the cemetery catty-corner across the street. The walls of the tunnel are supported by beams, some steel and some wooden. It also has wire fencing being used for support in some places on the wall. In the bunker that is her work area, there's loads of wires, a portable Centipede workbench with lab tops on top and generators underneath. It has a look of NASA's Mission Control. She takes her first positive dirt canister and connects it to a receptacle located on the ceiling directly under the vault of a coffin. Each vault has a receptacle located underneath it with thick wires creating electric highways to the work bench.

OFF SCREEN the song ends.

DISSOLVE TO
LONG SHOT of Jay's pickup truck cruising down the street.

OFF SCREEN the song "Put the Light on Me" by Brownville Station begins to play.

CUT TO

MEDIUM SHOT inside the truck of Jay, Greg, Al, and Tim. Their mini private retirement party is underway. The song gets quieter when they speak.

AL. When do we find out what we're doing?

TIM. Yes, we're getting a little nervous.

JAY. I believe when you retire, you need to turn back the clock and do something that you did before you started your careers.

GREG. That's almost forty years ago.

JAY. Yep, we had so much fun back then.

AL. I don't remember doing something long ago then thinking I'll do this again for my retirement party.

JAY. I didn't have a retirement party, so tonight is also mine. And Greg doesn't retire until this next year, so this is his preretirement party.

GREG. Wonderful, now, you got me nervous.

CUT TO

LONG SHOT of the truck getting closer to their destination, the local golf course, as the song gets loud again briefly.

CUT TO

MEDIUM SHOT of inside the truck again.

TIM. Oh no, we're not golf ball hunting, are we?

JAY. Yes, forty years ago, we were kind of poor because we were saving every dime from our summer jobs for college, so we had to do something to get spending money.

AL. And that was golf ball hunting. Did you bring trash bags?

GREG. We'll freeze.

JAY. No way, there's a hot spell this week.

TIM. Remember our dads taking the balls we found to where they work to sell?

JAY. They sold like hotcakes, and that was our summer spending money.

DISSOLVE TO
OFF SCREEN the song's volume increases still once again before eventually coming to an end.

SERIES OF SHOTS of the foursome in the golf course ponds submerging to gather lost balls on the mucky bottom and then coming back up for air. They repeat this routine until each person partially fills a trash bag.

The song ends with three out of the four treading water as they hold their trash bags.

JAY. I don't remember treading water while holding a trash bag of golf
    balls being so difficult.
GREG. I agree.
TIM. Where's Al?

Al then immediately and frantically emerges from under the water.

AL. Something slimy touched me. Let's get out of here!

All four rush for the shore each having difficulty with whatever stroke they chose. They clobber themselves in the head again and again due to one arm holding a trash bag partly filled with golf balls. Once on shore, they exhaustedly collapse completely out of breath.

AL. It had to be, it just had to be a Ditchman!
GREG. Are you sure?
JAY. I guarantee you it wasn't a Ditchman.

AL. I tell you something wrapped around my legs. Maybe then it was the hodag! These ponds have tributaries that flow into Grand Lake St. Marys, and that's where the hodag comes from.

JAY. The hodag is just a myth.

TIM. We responded to a lot of hodag sightings over the years.

AL. We sure did!

GREG. Really?

TIM. It seemed to mess around a lot with the picnic tables near Grand Lake.

JAY. I've heard enough. Let's get these bags to the truck.

The legend of the hodag in Grand Lake St. Marys began in the early 1900s. Although description varies, most reports describe it as about the same size of an elephant with a head of a horse and a body of a serpent. It has a hump on its back, chicken-like feet, a green eye on its forehead, and a red eye on its long ropelike tail. It is reported to have an eerie moan and a tendency to cackle when amused.

DISSOLVE TO

The foursome laughing and emptying their trash bags of golf balls into the bed of the pickup truck. They all then sit and rest on the edge of the truck bed going through the golf balls looking for the damaged ones.

JAY. Remember we need to get rid of the duds?

AL. We used to just toss them out as we drove down the street. We would hear an occasional bang or crash.

TIM. I can't believe we just did this. It does take you back and make you feel young again.

GREG. I don't remember being this out of breath after doing this. (*Pause as everyone agrees.*) You know it wasn't drugs or alcohol that made the 1970s wild. It was doing crazy fun things like this.

JAY. The last time we hunted for golf balls was my bachelor party. Remember, I promised Amy no alcohol at my bachelor party, and despite that, it still was one of the wildest of all time.

AL. How did you not lose your ostomy bag just now in the pond?

JAY. It's pasted to my body pretty good. That's why I always carry an extra one, except for today. They snap on and off like Tupperware.

AL. I knew all that. Sorry I asked. Your ostomy bag probably scared off the hodag.

JAY. Very funny.

CUT TO

LONG SHOT of Stevie in the distance in his Volkswagen and helmet driving down the road in route to deliver a pizza.

CUT TO

GREG. There goes Stevie delivering a pizza. Remember his dad, Stevie Senior?

TIM. It just dawned on me. Stevie Sr. died in a motorcycle crash on that very same road.

AL. Do you think that's why Stevie wears a helmet all the time?

JAY. Maybe. That would make sense.

GREG. He'd be proud how dependable Stevie turned out to be delivering pizzas.

TIM. Don't want to take away from the pizza places today, but what about the pizza places we had back in the day?

AL. If you would put them all together, they would have had the perfect pizza.

JAY. You're right. Leaning Tower's thick crust, La Grande's tasty sauce, the Pizza Shack's stretchy cheese, and Poppa Arties' fresh toppings.

AL. Toppings that our classmates who worked there would heave out of the back door if you were to drive your car around the rear of the building.

GREG. So much fun and memories. Then we started our careers and became serious adults. But we still had fun.

JAY. What about when we created a make-believe staff member, put their name on the PA announcements, and even gave them a mailbox? Then we made sure a student teacher got that name for Secret Santa Week. (*Pause until after laughter subsides.*) Or what about the time that we created fake sub plans?

GREG. Yes, we put in the plans to go out and count the number of vans being used for parent pickup as opposed to the number of cars.

JAY. And they did it! (*Then laughs hysterically.*)

GREG. Speaking of sub plans.

JAY. No.

GREG. Come on. I'm in a bind. I need one day language arts, one day science. It's Halloween Week. Teachers use their personal days.

JAY. This is it, no more, Greg. I'm retired.

AL. What's the big deal? It's just two days.

TIM. You go and just teach.

JAY. You don't just teach. Teaching is a performance. You couldn't get the Beatles back on the stage and expect them to be at the same level.

GREG. Yes, they would be a little rusty especially the dead ones.

JAY. The same goes for me. I will be rusty.

They start to climb out of the truck bed to leave.

AL. Speaking of subs, Tim's and mine's replacements aren't like us at all.

TIM. They are more controlling, not so hands off.

AL. Any surprises out of Amy's lab and they won't remain calm and cooperate like us.

TIM. They will look at it like an opportunity.

JAY. Oh boy, going from a couple of Sheriff Andy Taylors to a couple of Deputy Barney Fifes.

CUT TO

MEDIUM SHOT of the foursome inside the truck cab.

AL. We are going to be a lot sorer than we were forty years ago doing this. I got to join that new fitness-and-wellness center, whatever you call it.

GREG. That place was impressive.

TIM. And that Vance seemed like a great guy.

JAY. You're about the fifth person to tell me that today.

GREG. That Vance is a great guy.

JAY. Six.

AL. Honestly, the whole thing should be a real asset to the community.

DISSOLVE TO

Ted's old rural property in a Sunday morning, which now belongs to Vance.

CUT TO

Moving trucks in the driveway finishing unloading things into the house.

CUT TO

Vance standing in the driveway appreciating another beautiful sunny fall morning. This one happens to be a Sunday.

MOVER. That wraps it up, Mr. Wringer.

VANCE, *snapping out of it*. Call me Vance. Thanks for doing this on such short notice and on a Sunday to boot.

Vance then hands him a big tip for them all.

VANCE. Now, divide that among yourselves.
MOVER. No problem. Thank you, sir. Call us anytime. Enjoy your
    new home.
VANCE. I certainly will. Thank you.

Vance watches them depart his driveway onto the country road.

*Vance then walks slowly over to the area in his front yard near the fence
that parallels the ditch. He starts putting small marker flags into the
ground forming a rectangle that is perpendicular to the fence and the
ditch. Vance steps back and inspects his own work.*

CUT TO
*A familiar black SUV pulling into the driveway. Apparently, Vance
already has visitors.*

CUT TO
*Vance noticing the arrival of the black SUV and slowly makes his way
toward it.*

CUT TO
*Two SCUM agents slowly exiting the vehicle. SCUM stands for Special
Covert Unit Managers. They are dressed in their usual garbs, darks suits
and sunglasses. They still support long beards as well. They are a cross
between Men in Black and the Amish.*

*They move to square off with Vance. It appears confrontation is about to
take place.*

VANCE, *not in his usual friendly voice.* Bando said you'd be highly
    motivated.
SCUM AGENTS. We are.

VANCE. Well, you're no longer SCUM. You're farmhands, long-haired country boys. Go ahead. Put your stuff inside. Get changed. We got work to do.

Vance clearly is financially backed by defense contractor Stan Bando. He has been set up to infiltrate the community as a friendly, successful businessman. Stan Bando is obviously still interested in the Ditchmen research and is seeking vengeance for his failure fourteen months ago at the hands of Amy and Jay. Stan Bando still envisions Ditchmen as a potentially valuable weapon to mass produce.

DISSOLVE TO
Jay and Clay working in the bunker that they made under the more-modern cemetery located across the street and diagonal from Amy's lab. Clay continues removing dirt in a wheelbarrow, and Jay continues installing electric lines from the cement vaults suspended down from the bunker's ceiling to Amy's computer terminal workstation.

CLAY, *as he hauls dirt with a wheelbarrow.* You know I googled Vance Wringer.

JAY. You did? You know when I google someone, they usually die. I must be a jinx.

CLAY. No, you only google old movie and rock stars to see how old they are. So sure, they die shortly after. Anyways, did you know he has a degree in environmental science? And he wasn't that successful of a bodybuilder.

JAY. Interesting, are you sure this isn't about Debbie quitting college to work for him?

CLAY. No, it isn't about that.

JAY. Then how about some jams? It's Sunday morning, and instead of being in church, we are underneath a cemetery. So how about some country gospel?

Jay walks over to the workstation and turns on his Alexa, a voice-controlled virtual-assistant device.

OFF SCREEN "Heaven's Just a Sin Away" by the Kendalls begins to play.

CUT TO
Jay and Clay continue to work and sing along.

DISSOLVE TO
The new SCUM now dressed as farmhands with flannel shirts and ball caps, their beards shortened down to just a rugged look. They come out of the house to get their orders.

CUT TO
Vance who is near the area that he had flagged. SCUM INTO FRAME.

VANCE. Now, that's more like it. You won't stick out so much now.
SCUM AGENT #1. We're definitely more comfortable.
VANCE. Bando had a drone equipped with a lidar sensor fly over this area, which produces evidence of an anomaly right in this spot that I flagged. And that correlates with the local history of Simon Girty and his renegade raids that were also right here. So I need you to take the sod off and rototill. Then set up the generator. The mysterious runoff from the windmills and farms into ditches should then flow right into this space we made.
SCUM AGENT #2. Makes sense.
SCUM AGENT #1. Yep.
VANCE. I got to go into town and get a tour of some Canal Boat Museum. But then I am going to orchestrate a tour of Amy's lab and try to pick up some tips on how exactly she does this.

CUT TO
Jay and Clay no longer listening to any music as they continue working in the bunker.

JAY. Now, we need some music to energize us. Alexa, play "Chairman of the Board" by Chairmen of the Board.
ALEXA. Here's music by Frank Sinatra.
JAY. Clay! Get Alexa to play what I want.

CLAY. Wasn't Frank Sinatra nicknamed the Chairman of the Board?

JAY. Yes, but I want "Chairman of the Board" by Chairmen of the Board.

CLAY. But isn't that Frank Sinatra? Don't you like the Chairman of the Board?

JAY. Listen, I like Frank's music but not to do manual labor to. I need a song with some energy. I want "Chairman of the Board" by Chairmen of the Board. It's a funk song. Frank is not funky.

CLAY. But how can a song be the performer?

JAY. It just is. Listen, there's a song in 1970 called "Chairman of the Board" by a group that just so happens to be called Chairmen of the Board.

CLAY. Oh, okay, I'll see what I can do.

Clay walks over to the Alexa and makes some adjustments to Jay's request.

OFF SCREEN *the song "Chairman of the Board" by Chairmen of the Board begins to play.*

Jay and Clay continue working but now with more energy.

CUT TO

Amy eventually entering the bunker and turning off Alexa after watching them work and dance for a bit.

AMY. Nice dancing. We are going to have it quiet down here for a while.

JAY. Why?

AMY. Debbie just called. Guess who's coming over for a tour.

CLAY. Vance Wringer

AMY. That's right.

JAY. You okay?

AMY. Yes, I just wish that I'd kept my big mouth shut. There's just not much up there to show him. It's all down here, and I am certainly not going to show him this.

JAY. We'll stop down here and go work out back.

Amy gives them the thumbs up and then heads back toward the lab. Jay and Clay watch her depart. Then he turns and tells Alexa to resume the song. They start dancing again.

DISSOLVE TO
Amy leading Vance into the main lab. The tour has already begun.

AMY. This isn't going to be near as impressive as your open house. There's just not much to show.

VANCE. I don't need to see everything. I am mainly interested in your work. I know that you concluded that some kind of by-product from the windmills was going into the ground mixing with agricultural runoff in the ditches. Now, why was the cemetery so vital?

AMY. That's the unknown factor. It's impossible to prove scientifically what was mixing with the ditch buildup. I'd like to think, my hypothesis, it was the remnants of the souls from the rural cemetery out there. I determined this because when I was only able to create the same number of Ditchmen as there were bodies in that cemetery, Jay says it was my aura that triggered things. Sometimes, he thinks it might have also been the cinnamon that I was constantly putting on my applesauce cups. That's pretty much what I lived off of during my time in the bunker.

VANCE. Cinnamon?

AMY. Yes, I love putting it on everything. So Jay seems to think because of my love for it, the dirt was symbolically receiving part of me through the cinnamon, of course along with remnants of the souls in the cemetery, the agricultural runoff, and the windmill by-product. This all isn't an exact science.

VANCE. So you got this treated soil in the ditch that also gets contaminated by either your aura, the remnants of souls from the graves, or cinnamon because of your love for it. You're right. It's not an exact science. Sounds more like Harry Potter or the Adams Family.

They get near the temporal lobe display.

VANCE. This is interesting. It looks like an arcade game.
AMY. This is where I need your discretion. It isn't public knowledge yet, but that's a temporal lobe that was found in one of the last Ditchmen. One of its functions is to regulate emotion. I am using it as an experiment to see if I can enhance some of the ditch soil. It hasn't produced any results yet.

Vance looks on extremely interested despite Amy not being specific about her efforts to create and separate positive and negative dirt.

CUT TO
Amy suddenly receiving a message notification on her phone.

AMY. (*First out loud to herself then to Vance.*) You got to be kidding me. They know I'm busy. Excuse me. They need the key to the grader out back.
VANCE. No problem.

CUT TO
Amy leaving Vance alone and taking a key out the back door to Clay.

CUT TO
Vance very calmly helping himself to the canister that contains the negative enhanced dirt and hiding it up his jacket sleeve. It almost feels like a flashback of Dr. Frankenstein's assistant, Igor, selecting the abnormal brain instead of the normal one.

CUT TO
Amy out back giving Jay and Clay the key to the grader.

AMY. You know I'm busy in here giving Vance a tour.
JAY. Sorry, we didn't want to track mud everywhere.

CUT TO
Vance securing the canister before Amy returns.

CUT TO
Amy returning.

AMY. Sorry about that.
VANCE. No problem, I've enjoyed our little chat immensely. I feel
    very informed and up-to-date, so I'll let you get back to work. I
    appreciate you taking the time.
AMY. Thank you for your hospitality yesterday.
VANCE. I am on my way to another tour, your Canal Boat Museum
    downtown. I am going to make a donation.
AMY. That's so nice of you. This town is a historic canal town.
VANCE, *as he exits*. Science and history, my two favorite pastimes.

DISSOLVE TO
SERIES OF SHOTS of the high school inside and out Monday morning.

CUT TO
*Jay walking into the classroom under a chorus of cheers. He does his talk
show legend Johnny Carson routine having one hand trying to halt the
applause while the other hand is down low encouraging them to keep it
up.*

JAY. Thank you. Thank you. You're too kind.
STUDENT #1. Are you coming out of retirement?
JAY. No, no, your wonderful principal is just desperate for subs this
    week. I'm doing language arts today and science tomorrow. So
    let's get started. Today, I am going to do a lesson on points of
    view of narratives. Now, don't confuse these points of view with
    when point of view is used as a synonym for an opinion. We are
    talking about narratives, stories. There are three kinds of points
    of view. There is "first-person point of view." This is when the
    narrator is a character in the story. The next one is "third-per-
    son limited point of view." This is when the narrator is not a
    character in the story, and we know the inner thoughts of only
    one character. Finally, there is "third-person omniscient point of
    view." This is when the narrator is not a character in the story,

and we know the inner thoughts of more than one character. I have the three definitions on the board labeled *A*, *B*, and *C*, and you have index cards labeled *A*, *B*, and *C* on your desk. I will now tell three stories. After each story, you will guess which point of view it was in. Any questions?

CUT TO

STUDENT #2. What stories?

JAY, *very slowly at first.* The ones that I am about to tell you. I know you people are not used to someone standing in front of you telling a story, but I promise I will be more entertaining than anything on your phones.

The students react with jeers and cheers.

JAY. All right, here we go. Story number one. This Halloween Week, you have your traditional Rotary Halloween costume parade. Well, I was in that exact same parade over fifty years ago—same sponsor, same format, same route. And I was a competitive little cuss. I wanted to be in that parade for one reason, to win best costume in the category of scariest. My mother helped me make some strips out of a sheet and dressed me up as a mummy. I was now very confident that I would impress the judges and victory would be mine. So the parade started, and I had the mummy walk down pat. But not even a block into the parade, I started to unravel. And by a couple blocks, I had completely unraveled. I was now in the parade as myself. But I kept the mummy walk going in my street clothes, and I never lost hope of winning. Even despite such comments from the crowd as "nice costume" and "who are you supposed to be?" I remember then going past the judges and remaining determined despite the perplexed looks on their faces. And of course, I did not win but was very proud of my never-give-up attitude. (*Pause.*) Okay, let's now make a choice of which point of view that narrative was: *A*, first person; *B*, third person limited; or *C*, third person omniscient.

CUT TO
LONG SHOT of the class making their choices then raising their choices when Jay requests them to do so. Most of the choices were "A," first person point of view. Jay has them explain why it was first person and then begins the second narrative.

JAY. Now, our second story is a perfect one to tell since it is Halloween Week. There was this guy who was looking to buy a new home. This realtor was showing him this particular home. He was very anxious to move, so he didn't see much of the house before he decided to buy it. Well, the realtor was very conscientious, and she thought he needed to know that a monster supposedly lives in the basement. The guy was in disbelief of this information and even became suspicious that the women didn't want for some reason to sell him this house. So he demanded to buy it immediately. He didn't own a lot of stuff, so he was able to move in without even going down to the basement. It was a couple weeks after this that he was sitting in his living room watching TV. I believe it was *The Brady Bunch*.

CUT TO
Student #1 raising his hand with a question.

STUDENT #1. Who's the Brady Bunch?
JAY. Not that important. I forgot I'm old. Don't you know the theme song? Here's the story (*starting to sing somewhat*) of a lovely lady.

The students just give him blank stares.

JAY. Anyway, while he was watching TV, he remembered what the realtor had told him about a monster that lives in the basement. He thought to himself, *I'm going down there and seeing this monster for myself.* So downstairs he went—fifty steps to the right, fifty steps to the left. He looks around in a dark corner. He sees the monster and gets scared and runs back up and locks himself in his bedroom. Well, he was the type of person that could forget about his problems, so two weeks had gone by, and again, he was in the living room watching *The Brady Bunch*. (*Pause.*) If anyone asks me a question, I will give them detention for life. Now, as he watches TV this time, he thought to himself, *I am going downstairs, and this time, I am going to hit that monster for being in my basement.* So down the stairs he went, fifty steps to the right and fifty steps to the left. He walked up to the monster and raised his fist but then chickened out and ran back upstairs and locked himself in his bedroom. Again, a couple more weeks had gone by before the guy watching TV started to think about the monster in his basement. This time, I am going down there, and I am really going to hit that monster. Fifty steps to the right and fifty steps to the left. He runs to the monster and slugs it hard right in the shoulder. Then runs up and locks himself in his bedroom. The monster felt the pain of the blow to his shoulder, and it wasn't long before he started coming up the stairs, fifty steps to the left and fifty steps to the right. It's in the kitchen. It's in the dining room. It's in the bedroom, and it knocks down the bedroom door. It comes up to the guy and goes, "Tag you're it." (*Jay actually taps a male student at this point startling him.*)

The students react with cheers and jeers as Jay instructs them to choose which point of view this narrative was. Once again, most choose the correct answer, which is "C," third person omniscient. Jay goes on to point out that we knew the inner feeling of all three characters.

DISSOLVE TO

Vance at his newly purchased house inspecting the work done by his two farmhands, the former SCUM agents. The sod is gone in the rectangular area, and the ground is rototilled as well.

VANCE. Looks good. Now, we need to add this enhanced dirt that I confiscated from Amy Griner's lab.

The farmhands smile and give a small applause as Vance scatters the canister unbeknownst to him of negative enhanced dirt on top of the tilled area, which evidence points to be a burial ground for one of Simon Girty's pillage in the late 1700s.

VANCE. Now, let's connect this dirt to the generator and start giving it some juice.

The farmhands follow his directions hooking up the dirt pile like a car getting its battery a jump start.

FARMHAND #1 (*formerly SCUM agent #1*) Get ready to yell, "It's alive. It's alive!"

They stand back and wait and wait and wait. Nothing happens.

VANCE (*heading toward his vehicle*). No worries, I anticipated this, and I have a backup plan, thanks to Amy Griner. But it's not cinnamon.

CUT TO

The farmhands just looking at each other confused and shrugging their shoulders.

CUT TO

Vance coming back with a big square cardboard box and lets the farmhands know that there are a couple more boxes in his vehicle.

VANCE. This could just be what's missing.

FARMHAND #1. What is it?

VANCE. Something I just love, the Oreo bits used in my dirt cake recipe. Hopefully, it will provide my aura or my essence.

FARMHAND #1. Your what?

FARMHAND #2. Oreo bits, it looks like dirt.

VANCE. More like my dirt cake. Now, spread it out. (*Pause to watch.*) Let's hit the juice again.

The farmhands give this new pile a jolt from the generator and wait around for a while. There is no reaction from the dirt.

FARMHAND #1. Do you need to add the other ingredients from your dirt cake recipe like this box of gummy-worm packages?

VANCE. Go ahead. (*Looking up noticing it's getting dark.*) Maybe it just needs some time. Let's call it a night.

CUT TO

CLOSE-UP of the pile with the negative enhanced dirt on top and the Oreo bits on top sprinkled with gummy worms.

DISSOLVE TO

SERIES OF SHOTS a couple of hours later including the dark sky, the generator, Vance asleep in his bed, and the dirt pile.

CUT TO

CLOSE-UP of the dirt pile as just one large area in the middle begins to have one big percolation. This is completely different than the Ditchmen who each had two eyes percolating. Sure enough, the pile surges up revealing only one gigantic eye in the middle like some kind of cyclops. It slides and scoots a short way to the fence where two of the gummy worms come out. They give a thrust outward breaking open a portion of the fence. The gummy worms then disappear back into its midsection. It resembles an enormous scoop of dirt cake minus the pudding as it scoots from the ditch to the road.

OFF SCREEN is the background music from the 1964 Jonny Quest cartoons that played whenever a creature was moving about. As it heads toward town, a car approaches, and the Dirt Cake simply flattens itself entirely allowing the car to drive over, not even feeling like a speed bump as the music stops. It then rises back up into a giant moving scoop of Dirt Cake with one enormous dark percolating eye. The music resumes as down the road again it continues somewhat resembling a hovercraft.

CUT TO
MEDIUM SHOT of Vance sleeping away through it all.

DISSOLVE TO
SERIES OF SHOTS of the school on a Tuesday morning.

CUT TO
Leslie Greer Horn and Jay Griner crossing each other's path in the hall-way. Their conversations are so much pleasanter than they were a couple of years ago.

LESLIE. I would just love to be a fly on the wall today to watch you teach science.

JAY. Why, I am a lab assistant nowadays.

LESLIE. Isn't it difficult to make science lessons as unique as you made your language arts lessons?

JAY. Yes, it is more difficult but possible. (*Pause.*) I noticed in my sub plans that I have to monitor a study hall. I hope it is nothing like the old Study Hall 18 at the old high school building. That huge room with the antique desks.

LESLIE, *walking away.* Don't worry. It's not like Study Hall 18. Good luck. Have a nice day. Or wait, could you remind Amy about Friday night?

JAY. Friday night?

LESLIE. My Murder Mystery Winery Tour.

JAY. Oh yes that. Will do.

LESLIE. Ted's getting us a limo bus.

CUT TO

Vance dropped his morning coffee upon the discovery that something has been unleashed from his backyard.

CUT TO

Jay entering the still empty science classroom, as students start to come in. After some good mornings, the classroom quickly fills up, and everyone is seated.

JAY. I know, I know, it should be my wife teaching you science today. She did however help me set up this special Halloween Week science lesson last night. Now, you've been studying physics focusing on its basic vocabulary, acceleration, impact, and so on. Newton's laws of motion also has been introduced to you from what I understand. You need to first get those notes out. Next, you are going over to this box, and help yourself to a Ditchman cookie.

The students react with curiosity.

STUDENT #1. What's a Ditchman cookie?

JAY (*holding up a sugar cookie in the shape of a gingerbread man with green icing*). Here. It is merely a sugar cookie in the shape of a gingerbread man with green icing and red hots for eyes and mouth. So you get a cookie, look over all the different props, go back to your seat, and use your notes to create a type of contraption that will keep the Ditchman from the least amount of injury after we drop it out the window. But you need to write your plan out first using your physics vocabulary and any laws of motion before you actually make it. When I said props, that includes bubble wrap, Styrofoam peanuts, plastic grocery bags maybe for parachutes, and lots of other stuff to help create your apparatus.

STUDENT #2. Isn't this what they call the egg drop?
JAY. It would be if we were dropping eggs, but we are dropping Ditchmen. Another difference is the egg could be concealed, but the cookie cannot. Got that? You can't cover up the Ditchmen. This will force you to utilize more physics.

The students eagerly get started.

DISSOLVE TO
The finished products being dropped one at a time from the second-floor science room.

JAY. Remember, after we drop yours, you go down and get it and take it to our temporary triage to assess the damage. I see that one down there lost both of its legs. Let's hope your application of physics doesn't cause any decapitations.

SERIES OF SHOTS of more projects and their Ditchmen drops including school counselor Leslie Greer Horn enjoying the lesson and helping out.

DISSOLVE TO
LONG SHOT of a fast-food drive-through line. It is now Tuesday evening.

CUT TO
SERIES OF SHOTS of customers inside eating and staff working.

CLOSE-UP of the landscaping near the drive-through intercom. One area of the mulch looks a little darker and different.

OFF SCREEN that same eerie background music from the 1964 Jonny Quest cartoon series as before begins to play. Suddenly, the darker mulch, which in reality is Oreo dirt cake crumbs, begins to slowly rise, starting with the percolation of the one gigantic eye that looks like a case of black licorice bubble gum. There are currently no cars in the drive-through line as the enormous scoop of dirt cake displaying no arms or legs, just gummy-worm extensions, leans toward the intercom.

CUT TO
The worker inside not sure anyone is waiting to order.

WORKER. (*First to his coworkers around.*) Is there someone waiting to order?

CUT TO
The Dirt Cake at the intercom.

WORKER. (*Voice over intercom.*) Your order, please.

The Dirt Cake then gives a bloodcurdling howl that could best be described as a combination of a Bigfoot scream and Lloyd's most annoying sound in the world form the movie Dumb and Dumber.

CUT TO
SERIES OF SHOTS of customers and workers reacting in complete panic and fear to the noise blasting from the intercom. Food is spilled or dropped from trays. Some customers even duck under their tables. One small hand is shown reaching back up to grab a french fry.

CUT TO

The giant scoop of Dirt Cake scooting down the empty street and into the darkness.

CUT TO

The scared drive-through worker slowly rising up and making his way to the microphone.

WORKER: Please pull up to the window.

CUT TO

A nearby park where a lighted horseshoe court exists. The Tuesday Night League, consisting mostly of septuagenarians and a few octogenarians, is busy pitching their horseshoes.

CUT TO

CLOSE-UP of a light pole with an electric cable leading up to a power lever switch.

INTO FRAME the Dirt Cake rises up the light pole like the pile of ooze in the movie The Blob. *One of its gummy-worm limbs extends slowly out and pulls the switch turning off the court's lights. Everything becomes completely dark.*

OFF SCREEN the voices of the horseshoe players can be heard.

PLAYER #1. Should we stop?
PLAYER #2. Absolutely not.
PLAYER #3. It's just a little ole blackout, and we're so close to finishing this game.
PLAYER #4. Come on. Pitch!

After a few moments of darkness, horseshoes are heard landing and bouncing. Next, what is heard are the moans and cries of the players. So are they being struck by horseshoes or attacked by Dirt Cake? The lights soon get turned back on by one of the players. The other players are shown holding their hurt shins. There is no sign of Dirt Cake.

DISSOLVE TO

SERIES OF SHOTS Wednesday morning of the city's Memorial Park, including its covered bridge, bell tower, flagpole, cannons, and the Canal Boat Museum.

CUT TO

Vance walking slowly in the park near the Canal Boat Museum that rests on the canal waters. He is carefully looking at the mulch. Vance is evidently looking for the Dirt Cake creature realizing it can flatten itself into a plant bed. Bits of Oreo cookie would be a tip that it is hiding there.

CUT TO

The lady museum curator spotting Vance as she walks to work.

CURATOR. Good morning, Mr. Wringer.

VANCE. Good morning, ma'am. Is this new mulch?

CURATOR. Heavens no, we won't waste all that money you donate to us on something as mundane as mulch.

VANCE. Oh, I wasn't worried about that. You're welcome to use it any way you see fit. I was just admiring all the landscaping in the park.

CUT TO

Vance's two farmhands walking about a neighborhood filled with very nice and rather large older homes. They are also looking closely at mulched landscapes. Suddenly, they almost collide with a passerby. It is an older man still blessed with dark hair with a nice part. He is wearing horn-rimmed glasses with very thick lenses. The collision almost occurs because the man isn't paying attention to where he is going, but instead, he is busy whistling to the birds in the trees. The two farmhands just shake their head at each other and continue walking. It isn't long before another collision occurs with another passerby. This time, it is an old lady named Esther adorn with a straw hat, a bit of a goatee, and a bathrobe over her nightie. She is meticulously busy sweeping the sidewalks. Her eyes are oddly gawking straight ahead and not down at the sidewalk. One of the farmhands seems impatient and starts toward the lady before being pulled back by the other farmhand.

FARMHAND #1. Never mind her.
FARMHAND #2. Her? She looks like the Quaker Oats guy.

As they come upon the next house, they are immediately greeted by a very vocal elderly woman who first has some choice words for the old lady sweeping the sidewalks.

ELDERLY WOMAN. Esther! Watch where in the tarnation you're sweeping. You just about hit my landscapers. (*Then she turns to the two farmhands.*) Don't mind her. She's either an angel disguised as a stranger, or just plain bats. Every day, she sweeps every sidewalk in town. You two sure got here quickly. I really do appreciate that. (*She waves for them to follow her.*) I can't believe I didn't notice it before.

FARMHAND #1. I'm sorry ma'am, but you must have mistaken us…

She takes them to the side of her house.

ELDERLY WOMAN, *interrupting.* A big pile of black mulch right in the middle of my red mulch.

The two farmhands just take a quick look at each other realizing this may be what they are looking for. They decide not to correct the elderly woman for mistaken their identity.

FARMHAND #1. That's our bad. We'll get that out of there for you.

FARMHAND #2. Right away, ma'am.

ELDERLY WOMAN. You go ahead and get started removing the black mulch, and I will go get you some ice-cold lemonade.

The two farmhands slowly approach the dark mulch, which just happens to resemble Oreo crumbs. Just as they lean down toward it, Dirt Cake emerges up and out of the plant bed leaving it to be solely red mulch.

CUT TO

CLOSE SHOT of the two farmhands as their eyes widen and their mouths drop open. They then jump backward taking off running toward the front yard with Dirt Cake scooting right behind. They run right by the elderly woman coming around the front with a tray of lemonade.

ELDERLY WOMAN. Your lemonade! (*Pause to go back inside.*) Wow, they don't even use a wheelbarrow nowadays. The mulch just follows them right out of the yard.

OFF SCREEN Molly Hatchet's "Flirtin' with Disaster" plays briefly as Dirt Cake continues his pursuit of the farmhands. At the first sign of any traffic, it dissipates at the base of a nearby tree. Once the coast is clear, it pops up again. Using its one eye and most of its blob-like body, it veers to the right and then to the left before scooting on. Once again, as soon as a sign of life appears, it dissipates into the nearest bare spot or mulch bed.

LONG SHOT of this routine repeating a couple more times. Dirt Cake even has his gummy-worm limbs appear briefly to help make quicker turns from one side to the other to see if anyone is in sight. These quick turns resemble John Belushi outside the sorority house in the movie Animal House.

DISSOLVE TO
LONG SHOT of a couple of police officers slowly walking up to the front door of Amy's lab on a Wednesday morning. They press her door-buzzer button.

CUT TO
Amy opening the door.

AMY. (*Obviously to her surprise.*) Good morning, officers. May I help you?

OFFICER #1. Sorry to bother you, Mrs. Griner, but we had couple of strange incidents last night that frankly sound very Ditchman-like.

AMY. So every time something strange happens in town, you are going to assume it's my lab that's causing it.

OFFICER #1. But, Mrs. Griner, as I said, these incidents were very Ditchman-like.

AMY. Well, my research is going nowhere. You are welcome to come in and have a look. See for yourself.

OFFICER #1, *as they enter.* Maybe a little look-see.

CUT TO
Jay and Clay parked by Vance's home near where the fence has been knocked down. They are busy examining the dirt area. Jay pauses to answer his phone.

JAY. (*On his phone.*) What's up?
AMY. (*OFF SCREEN.*) The police were here.
JAY. The police?

CUT TO
AMY. There was evidently a couple of strange things that happened last night, so naturally, they blame me and the Ditchmen, who

don't exist. Luckily, they didn't go down to the basement. At first, I thought they were here to arrest me for all that misinformation I gave Vance about cinnamon being what triggered the Ditchmen to come alive.

CUT TO

JAY. Amy, there's no such thing as the science police. How would they even know that you gave Vance a bunch of bologna about cinnamon being what made the Ditchmen come alive because you like putting it on applesauce so much. (*Breaking out laughing.*) That still cracks me up. Hey, Clay and I are looking right at evidence that something strange might have really happened recently.

AMY. (*OFF SCREEN.*) What?

JAY. I'm on my way! I'll fill you in when I get there, and we'll cover up that tarp area better in the basement just in case they come back.

He puts away his phone and waves to Clay to come to his vehicle.

CLAY. What's up? And what does all this mess mean?

JAY. Looks like Vance is in the Ditchmen business. Let's get out of here before he comes home from the fitness center.

DISSOLVE TO

SERIES OF SHOTS of the Grand Lake Cornhole Club building where the Wednesday-evening league is getting underway. Members file out of the facility (a large old storage building) after their brief meeting inside. Due to the pleasant weather, they begin playing outside, about six matches all at once. The competition is fun with some good-hearted barbs at each other.

CUT TO

Cornhole member Kimberli cheering on her cornhole partner and husband, Roger.

Kᴉᴍʙᴇʀʟɪ (*as he pitches multiple bags into the hole*) That's it, honey! Awesome pitch!

CUT TO
CLOSE SHOT of the cornhole board and it is obvious that the bare spot in the lawn is kind of darker than normal.

CUT TO
Kimberli reaching in to retrieve the bags when her arm is suddenly pulled in up to her shoulder. She screams hysterically. The Cornhole Club members all run to her rescue, but when the Dirt Cake lets go of Kimberli's arms and rises up to its full size tossing the cornhole board off to the side, the members immediately retreat. The Dirt Cake chases after them releasing that same horrid yell that it used at the drive-through intercom. As it uses its gummy limbs to heave the bags of corn at the players, everyone escapes, and the Dirt Cake appears to lunge into the bed of an extremely loud pickup truck speeding down the nearby street.

CUT TO

The driver of the pickup is dressed in a Halloween costume. He's dressed as Dr. Creep with skull-face make up and a black top hat with a dark cape. He doesn't even take his eye off the road.

DISSOLVE TO
Vance standing outside his fitness/wellness center as the farmhands pull up in a pickup truck, not their black SCUM SUV.

Vᴀɴᴄᴇ. Have you been listening to the police scanner?

FARMHAND #1. Yep, that had to be the Dirt Cake at the Cornhole Club. We drove by, but it was long gone.

FARMHAND #2. One of the persons there said something large threw itself into the back of Dr. Creep's truck.

FARMHAND #1. Whatever that means.

VANCE. Dr. Creep is a popular Tugfest contestant. I heard people at the center talking about him just today. And there's a Tugfest tonight! Get going. Find out where they have it. Keep me posted.

DISSOLVE TO

Amy, Jay, and Clay having an important discussion at the lab as they do a walk through.

AMY. So that's the way it's going to be. They'll come here every time something strange happens.

JAY. You said they didn't go to the basement. We were lucky.

AMY. Right. This time.

CLAY. We're pretty much finished under the cemetery. All the cables are connected to the cement coffin vaults. They're just waiting on your positive canisters to be connected to their receptacles. There's only one so far.

JAY, *to Clay.* That's what's stumping me. How did Vance create something? He didn't have all the components.

AMY. That reminds me. Do either of you have my negative canister? I can't seem to find it.

Jay and Clay immediately look at each other.

CLAY. Vance

AMY. Vance? He wouldn't.

JAY. He would. He did. Clay was right all along.

AMY. I can't believe he took that canister right under my nose. Let's go get it back from him.

JAY. Not yet, Amy.

AMY. Why not?

JAY. We don't know what we're dealing with yet. We need you to drop
   Clay and me off at his house. His fitness center is still open, so
   we should be able to snoop around some more.

DISSOLVE TO

*An open field near the edge of town where the traditional Halloween
Tugfest is about to begin. It is a unique event with a unique layout. The
spectators back their vehicles up side by side forming an oval in a big
field with one end open. This open end is where the participants gather
with pickup trucks. Nearby, there are porta potties and food vendors. The
pickup trucks compete two at a time in a single elimination tug-of-war-
like event. Facing the opposite direction, they are connected by a chain
or rope. They then try to each pull a flag across separate finish lines. The
spectators sit in lawn chairs near or in the bed of their pickup trucks
and cheer on their favorite drivers who are dressed tonight in various
Halloween costumes and names.*

*SERIES OF SHOTS of the Tugfest taking place. Dr. Creep with his top hat,
pale-painted face, and darken eyes easily has a victory. Wild Bill Fury
with his big bushy unibrow gets out of his vehicle after being defeated
and covers his ears as the crowd cheers on "Headless Lamarr," a female
driver whose costume is design to look like a headless woman but still
with the ability to drive.*

CUT TO

*The two farmhands showing up at the Tugfest. They park away from the
rest and walk up.*

FARMHAND #2. Why did you park so far away?
FARMHAND #1. I wasn't actually sure what we are getting ourselves
   into.
FARMHAND #2. It's a Tugfest. We've been to truck events before.
FARMHAND #1. Not one in an open field.

CUT TO

SERIES OF SHOTS of Dr. Creep preparing to go up against Headless Lamarr. They rev up their engines, and the crowd revs up their support.

CUT TO

CLOSE-UP of the bed of Dr. Creep's truck, which contains that strange very-dark soil. The soil then starts to fall out of the truck onto the ground between them without the aid of gravity. From that pile, Dirt Cake suddenly arises letting out its screeching, annoying cry. It's gummy-worm arms grab onto the cable or whatever connects the two vehicles. It seems to have the ability to increase its size. Both trucks start losing their attempt to tug as Dirt Cake continues yelling and pulling to the point that both vehicle's back ends rise up off the ground. The crowd simultaneously becomes terrified at this sight and immediately makes their getaway.

CUT TO

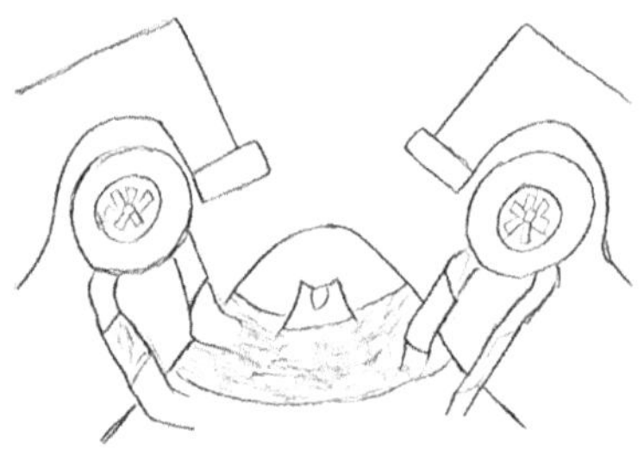

The two farmhands walking toward the Tugfest suddenly notice that every truck's headlights are coming straight for them. They make daring attempts to dodge the oncoming traffic as horns honk and lawn chairs and coolers fly out the back. Luckily, the two farmhands come out unscathed. There is a pause in their dodge dance as Dr. Creep and Headless Lamarr are the last two to zoom by.

CUT TO

The Dirt Cake as it plows into one end of the row of porta potties sending them sliding altogether like a choo choo with a few passengers jumping out.

CUT TO

The Dirt Cake appearing to be catching its breath. It then fixes his massive eye onto the two farmhands and begins his charge.

CUT TO

The farmhands attempting to accelerate toward their truck. After appearing to run in place for the first couple of seconds, they eventually get going and make it to their truck. They cleverly circle back around in the field and end up being in pursuit of Dirt Cake instead of being the prey.

CUT TO

Amy pulling up near the driveway of Vance's new home. Jay and Clay quickly get out and make their way toward the house. Jay stops when he notices the black SUV parked obviously hidden from view along with a couple of generators.

Jay. (*Pointing.*) Look familiar?
Clay. SCUM!
Jay. *Shh.*

They quietly enter and immediately notice there is very little furniture.

Clay. Hardly any furniture for someone settling down here.
Jay. Good observation.

Jay opens a door and notices nothing but a couple of sleeping bags in the room.

Jay. Just sleeping bags for SCUM I bet.
Clay. That other room must be Vance's. It at least has a bedroom suite, brand-new. Now, what do we do?
Jay. I believe we established they are here to hijack Amy's research. Stan Bando must be involved with this. He'll do nothing to stop trying to make weapons out of Ditchmen. That would explain SCUM being here and the generators. So there is only one thing to do. We send a message.

CLAY. And what will that accomplish?

JAY. It will make them nervous, on edge.

CLAY. What exactly are we going to do?

JAY. We are going to take his bedroom suite apart and put it back together in his driveway.

CLAY, *chuckling.* Are you kidding?

JAY. No, I'm dead serious. This will let him know that his cover is blown. Come on.

They then begin to slowly take Vance's bed apart and move it to the driveway, where they put it back together. They do the same with Vance's dresser and nightstand. Jay then gets his cell phone out and calls Amy to pick them up as they giggle and make their way to the end of Vance's driveway.

CLAY, *in between his giggles.* Pleasant dreams.

CUT TO

The two farmhands in their pickup truck in close pursuit of Dirt Cake. They are bumping it from behind as it turns and hastily slithers into a trailer park like an upside-down tornado.

CUT TO

Stevie inside his trailer on his couch having an evening snack and watching TV. His trusty helmet is nearby on his coffee table.

CUT TO

Dirt Cake basically being shoved from behind by the farmhands right into the side of Stevie's trailer.

CUT TO

Stevie being knocked off his couch by the jolt.

CUT TO

The farmhands repeatedly backing up and then ramming Dirt Cake again and again into the side of Stevie's trailer. It lets out bellows of agony.

CUT TO
Stevie getting up and then falling again as he reaches for his helmet as the jolts to his trailer continue.

STEVIE. Tornado! It's a tornado! And I'm in a trailer!

CUT TO

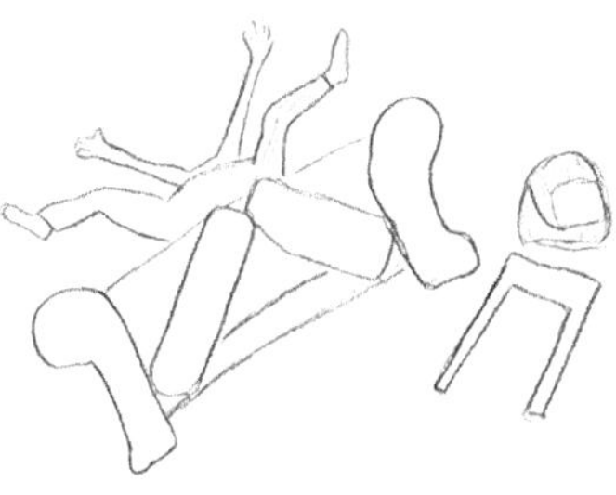

Dirt Cake regrouping and getting his bearings as it now begins to shove the truck backward right out of the trailer court crashing it into a nearby business storefront, which fortunately is closed.

CUT TO
Stevie rushing outside looking up at the screaming tornado. His volume eventually decreases as he realizes that it may not have been what he had first thought.

CUT TO
The Dirt Cake slithering its way right into the cemetery near Amy's lab.

DISSOLVE TO
Vance pulling into his driveway. He slowly gets out stunned by his bedroom suite situated in his driveway. The two farmhands that he had picked up also slowly get out.

VANCE. What is this? Who did this?
FARMHAND #1 (*to Farmhand #2*). That's still better than our sleeping
    arrangements.

The exhausted farmhands continue on inside. Vance just stands and resumes his amazement at his bedroom suite being in his driveway.

DISSOLVE TO
Thursday morning as Jay and Amy are driving toward town. They approach Vance's house.

CUT TO
MEDIUM SHOT of Vance still asleep in his bed in his driveway.

CUT TO
Jay and Amy breaking out into a hysterical laugh.

DISSOLVE TO
Jay and Amy now arriving at her lab.

CUT TO
The same two police officers as before waiting at the door.

AMY. Good morning, officers. Would you like another tour?
OFFICER #1. Sorry, Mrs. Griner, we better. There were more incidents last night.
JAY. You might want to try a tour of the new fitness-slash-wellness center.

The officers just look at Jay confused as they enter.

JAY. You really should.

DISSOLVE TO
Thursday night, the second biggest night of Halloween Week. Some would argue the most important night of the week. The tradition of trick-or-treating is about to take place.

SERIES OF SHOTS of the trick-or-treating night including scores of youngsters beginning to go door-to-door. One door belongs to Mr. Macamee, the Back in the Day Days emcee. He carefully examines each trick-or-treater and attempts to guess who they are dressed as, not even coming close to some obvious ones. Ted and Leslie set up outside their house passing out not only candy but also campaign material and items. His opponent, Woody Burns, is passing out treats in front of his great big obviously expensive billboard. It consists of a photo of himself and the slogan, "Had Enough Living in Fear? Vote for Woody Burns, He Promises to Keep You Safe!"

CUT TO

CLOSE-UP of a big bowl of small bags of potato chips with a sign that reads "Take one."

CUT TO

MEDIUM SHOT of COACH in his backyard grilling steaks.

SERIES OF SHOTS continue with Vance outside his fitness center preparing bowls of dirt cake for trick-or-treaters.

CUT TO

"Mutt Sitters," a dog day care business where employees are passing out kids' treats, dog treats, and flyers promoting that they will be open this Saturday during the Ghost Ball and the mayor's debate. The locations for both events just happen to be next door and across the street.

CUT TO

Jay, Amy, Clay, and Debbie setting up for trick-or-treaters just outside of Amy's lab.

JAY. I got to tell you I'm not crazy about doing this. It brings back some not-so-pleasant memories. My mom, the greatest mom, was a real stickler when it came to trick or treat. If she thought you were too old, she'd tell ya. If she thought you didn't have enough of a costume on, she'd tell ya. If you didn't say, "Thank you," she'd tell ya. I dreaded the next day at school when kids

would come up to me and tell me about my mom getting on
them.

AMY, *after laughing.* Well, I do appreciate everyone helping. We never
have anybody stop out in the country.

DEBBIE, *to Clay after he tells her something.* I knew it. I knew it. You
not being insecure about my new job was too good to be true.

CLAY. All I said was I don't trust him.

DEBBIE. He's so nice and a great boss. How could you not trust him?
You trust him, Jay, don't you?

JAY. Who?

DEBBIE. Vance, my boss. Clay doesn't trust him.

JAY. Oh, him, I don't trust him.

DEBBIE, *stunned.* Amy?

AMY. I don't trust him. We're pretty certain he stole something from
my lab and is conducting his own experiments. I'd been shut
down today if it wasn't for Jay and Clay's cover-up job in the
basement.

DEBBIE, *more stunned.* What?

AMY. I tell you what. Jay and Clay, why don't you take care of the
trick-or-treaters, and I'll take Debbie inside and get her updated
on things.

DEBBIE. Updated?

JAY, *sarcastically.* Wonderful.

CUT TO

*SERIES OF SHOTS of trick-or-treaters enjoying going door-to-door. Ted and
Leslie busy passing out their goodies, as well as Vance handing out bowls
of dirt cake. Mr. Macamee still having trouble guessing who trick-or-
treaters are dressed as.*

CUT TO

*The two farmhands in a different vehicle pulling up near Woody Burns's
billboard, where he is busy passing treats and campaign items.*

CUT TO

Woody Burns noticing that the farmhands had pulled up. He leaves his stand to his volunteers and makes his way near their vehicle.

Woody, *leaning in toward them with a loud whisper.* Tell your boss, "Thanks for the billboard!"

Farmhand #1. Remember that was an anonymous donation.

Woody, *putting his finger near his mouth shushing himself.* Right, gotcha.

CUT TO

Amy's bunker underneath the cemetery. Dirt Cake maneuvers his way around eventually finding himself at Amy's main terminal workstation. His gummy arms begin the process of turning everything on and starting up Amy's new experiment despite the fact that there is only one positive canister attached to a vault. Also, the Dirt Cake appears to turn the power to full capacity. The sound of surges flowing through the cables to hundreds of cemetery vaults. This exhilarates the Dirt Cake who bellows out one of his horrid cries. Amy and Debbie coming out of the tunnel into the bunker entrance spotting the Dirt Cake.

OFF SCREEN *the extended version of "Rain" by the Cult begins to play.*

CUT TO

CLOSE-UP *of the positive canister attached to a vault shaking violently.*

SERIES OF SHOTS *of the cemetery graves shaking and the vaults beginning to break through the surface.*

OFF SCREEN *the song continues then gets a little quieter for a brief moment.*

CUT TO

JAY, *to the trick-or-treaters.* I didn't hear a thank-you. (*Pause.*) Aren't you a little too old for this? (*pause*) That's not much of a costume. Oh my gosh, I'm turning into my mother.

CUT TO

Amy and Debbie running out from her lab to where Jay and Clay are busy with trick-or-treaters.

AMY. We saw it! We saw it!
JAY. Saw what?
DEBBIE. It's a giant piece of dirt cake!
CLAY. Dirt cake? More like earthquake!

CUT TO

LONG SHOT from Amy's lab's parking lot as the ground shakes and projectiles shoot out of the cemetery like rockets leaving a battleship. The song's volume increases.

JAY. The corpses! They're launching! Come on, Clay.
AMY. Oh my gosh, try and stop it! Hurry!

They rush inside to race to the cemetery through the tunnel in the lab's basement.

CUT TO

SERIES OF SHOTS of bodies blasting into the air from the open vaults as they completely lift out of the ground with pieces of exploding coffins land nearby. The first of hundreds.

CUT TO

Jay and Clay running into the bunker only to turn and retreat when they come face-to-face with the bellowing Dirt Cake.

LONG SHOT of the night skies. OFF SCREEN the song changes to "Raindrops Keep Fallin' on My Head" by B. J. Thomas.

CUT TO

SERIES OF SHOTS of trick-or-treaters in different parts of town stopping their fun to look up.

SERIES OF SHOTS of the incoming corpses and other contents from the coffins—hats, cigars, bowling balls, fishing poles, guitars, and golf clubs. One by one, they crash-land into the ground just missing the terrified trick-or-treaters. One lands destroying Woody Burns's new billboard.

CUT TO

Mr. Macamee trying to guess the costume of the corpse that landed on his front porch.

MR. MACAMEE. Uh, you're Rip Van Winkle? Jimmy Hoffa?

CUT TO

Another smashes in Vance's fitness/wellness center parking lot, prompting Vance to frantically look at it concluding that it is indeed a corpse.

CUT TO

One woman's corpse lands with her entire shoe collection that she had buried with her.

CUT TO

Another corpse lands right on Coach's steaks as he grills them. Coach snatches his bag of potato chips saving it from any damage.

COACH. Honey! I'm going to need a bigger spatula. (*Pauses.*) Why, it's our old neighbor, Shorty. Didn't he die years ago?

CUT TO

A very young trick-or-treater summing up what's happening.

YOUNG TRICK-OR-TREATER. It's storming zombies.

Almost an accurate account except these bodies do absolutely nothing once they hit the ground.

SERIES OF SHOTS of more corpses falling and more trick-or-treaters scattering. Corpses land in a swimming pool, through a roof interrupting an elderly couple watching Alfred Hitchcock's The Birds, *and through the windshield of the vehicle that the two farmhands are driving. One lands right in front of a woman as she opens her front door to see what all the screaming is about.*

CUT TO

CLOSE-UP of the corpse with the positive canisters sailing right with it.

CUT TO

LONG SHOT of the corpse and canister crashing into the turf football field at the high school.

CLOSE-UP of the broken positive canister and dirt spilled all over the turf field.

OFF SCREEN the song ends.

CUT TO
SERIES OF SHOTS of the corpses and the damage they caused all over town along with the curiosity seekers and first responders.

Amy, Jay, Clay, and Debbie assessing the damage in the bunker. There is no sign of Dirt Cake. Open holes to the above cemetery are all over the place.

AMY. What in the world happened here?

JAY. That dirt-cake-looking thing did this.

CLAY, *to Debbie.* You see, there is a disturbed dirt area near the ditch at Vance Wringer's house, and this creature looks like a giant bowl of the stuff he makes.

AMY. How did it launch corpses straight out their coffins and vaults? That's insane!

JAY. Lots of juice. Lots and lots of juice. We gotta fill in this bunker and tunnel right away. You know we're going to get blamed for all of this.

AMY. You're right. And my positive canister is missing.

JAY. It got launched with a corpse. It could be anywhere in town. We can't look now. This has to be done first.

CLAY. I'll get started.

DISSOLVE TO
Friday morning as Clay and Jay mop the basement area in front of the storage room door that contained the entry tunnel to the bunker.

JAY, *exhausted.* There, that should do it.

CLAY, *also exhausted.* I'm beat. We worked the entire night.

Amy INTO FRAME entering the basement.

AMY. Gentlemen, we have a problem.

CLAY. Police here already?

AMY. No, protesters, blaming us for last night. (*Pause.*) What's really odd is I pretty much know everybody in town, and I don't recognize a soul out there.

JAY. They got to be paid protesters. It's got to be Vance doing damage control because he lost that dirt-cake thing he created.

AMY. Their signs are so stupid. "Burn the Bigfoot Lab." "Rid this town of Mrs. Frankenstein."

CLAY. How do we get out of here?

AMY. There's nothing here I'm worried about. The temporal lobe is secure enough here.

JAY. We are parked out back. We just need a diversion.

DEBBIE. I have an idea, but I'll have to sneak around to the front.

DISSOLVE TO

Debbie walking toward the protestors from the side of the building opposite of the driveway leading to the back parking lot. As soon as she gets close enough, she holds up a bunch of coupons for a free dirt cake.

DEBBIE. Who didn't get their free dirt-cake coupons?

All the protestors immediately head toward Debbie excited about getting their free coupon.

CUT TO

Jay driving from behind the lab with Amy as his passenger. Clay is right behind them in his blue Chevy Nova.

DISSOLVE TO

Jay and Amy a few minutes later as they near their farmhouse. They slow down when they notice deputy sheriffs knocking at their door. They do a U-turn without being noticed and start back toward town.

AMY. Where are we headed?

JAY. Ted and Leslie's. I'm supposed to make sure he doesn't mess up Leslie's transportation plans tonight.

AMY. She's going all out for this Murder Mystery Winery Tour. It's not the best timing. It's an eighties' theme, and I've been assigned Toni Basil, "Oh, Mickey, you're so fine. You're so fine. You blow my mind, hey, Mickey. Hey, Mickey." Luckily, Debbie brought me one of her old cheerleading outfits last night. It's in the backseat thank goodness.

JAY. I might be taking a nap in that backseat soon.

AMY. What about that thing out there that I didn't create?

JAY. You mean Dirt Cake?

AMY. Dirt Cake? That's what we're going to call it?

JAY. It makes sense. Vance created it. He loves dirt cake, and it actually looks like giant scoop of the stuff.

DISSOLVE TO
Coach taking a stroll on his high school turf field the morning of tonight's big football game. The only people nearby are the proper local officials finishing putting the corpse that landed on the field into a body bag.

COACH, *as they walk by.* My wife has a spatula that works pretty good on those things. (*Coach then notices the broken canister and spilled dirt on the field. He starts to spread it out with his foot when it suddenly appears to be absorbed into the turf. He quickly bends down and attempts to pick some of it up, but the pieces of dirt escape his hand before he could examine it. Coach pops back completely baffled and appears to put on his thinking cap.*)

DISSOLVE TO
Jay and Amy at Ted and Leslie's house having breakfast.

TED. So my entire campaign is under attack by outsiders?

JAY. It appears so. My guess is Stan Bando financed Vance Wringer to hijack Amy's research and acquire control of your office.

AMY. I'm so sorry you're being linked to me.

TED. I don't care about losing the election. It's what they might do if their plan is successful that I am worried about. I got that debate tomorrow night. Amy, I'd like you to be there so we can present sort of a united front.

LESLIE. Oh, Ted, I don't think I've been prouder of you than I am right now. You guys, I got to go to work.

She gives Ted a peck on the cheek.

LESLIE. Now, is my limo bus ready for tonight?

TED. I confirmed the rental again yesterday. I go pick it up in a couple of hours.

LESLIE. And, Amy, you need a night out. Do you have your costume?

AMY. I look so fine, hey, Mickey.

Amy's phone rings, and she answers it.

AMY. Yes, you're kidding. You're kidding. Thanks so much for calling. I'm on my way. (*Pauses and then turns to everyone.*) Jay, we got to get to the football field, right away.

DISSOLVE TO
LONG SHOT of the Canal Boat Museum as it rests on the actual water of the canal.

CUT TO
CLOSE-UP of the mulch in the landscaped area near the museum. The camera PANS to the part of the mulch that is obviously much darker than the rest. It also has the texture of crumbled pieces of the chocolate-wafer part of an Oreo cookie. Dirt Cake is evidently doing his temporary hibernating right here. His one big eye even starts to percolate a little bit.

DISSOLVE TO
Coach, Jay, Amy, and Ted examining the turf field at the high school.

AMY, *kneeling down holding the canister.* I sure do appreciate you calling me.

COACH. What can I say? I prefer being part of your team.

AMY. You actually saw the dirt filter into the turf?

COACH. Yes, I did. It was as if they were running away from me. Very creepy.

AMY. Coach, I need someone to stake out this turf.

COACH. I'd like to help you with that, but I got a game to win tonight. My boys are ready.

AMY. Well, I am going to be a cheerleader tonight unfortunately, not here.

TED. And I am going to be your chauffeur.

JAY. Looks like I'm your huckleberry, or should I say huckle bearer, which is what is actually said in the movie meaning pallbearer back in those days.

AMY. Is that all right if we give Jay a camera and he can pretend to be a photographer?

COACH. Sure. I'm just glad Jay's not going to be the cheerleader. He's dangerous with pom-poms.

JAY. Not my proudest moment, Coach.

TED, *answering his cell phone, which the ringtone happens to be "Hail to the Chief."* What? You're kidding. There's nothing you can do? Are you sure? I understand. (*Turns to the rest.*) The limo bus for tonight is broken down. What am I going to do? Leslie will be devastated.

AMY. I'll say.

JAY, *walking away*. Come on. I got an idea.

AMY. You need to get back here as soon as you can.

JAY. I will. I will. See ya, Coach. Good Luck tonight!

COACH. Thank you kindly! My boys are ready to get on the field.

TED. What could possibly take the place of a limo bus?

JAY. We're going to have to replace quality with atmosphere.

TED. What does that mean?

DISSOLVE TO

OFF SCREEN Ian Hunter's live version of "Just Another Night" begins to play for a brief time.

SERIES OF SHOTS of early Friday evening around town including cleanup still taking place at the cemetery and dog pickups at the Mutt Sitter dog day care. Protesters still protesting at Amy's lab. Fans entering the high school football stadium ahead of the big game and Leslie's guests arriving at her house.

The song ends after showing a group of Boy Scouts along with their scout masters waiting near a plank that connects the historic Canal Boat Museum to the shore. They notice a replica of a mule that towed the canal boat. They are greeted by a tour guide who begins to spill out a lot of background information. A couple of the boys are not too happy about being there as they walk across the plank onto the boat.

BOY SCOUT #1. I can't believe we're missing the football game for this.
BOY SCOUT #2. Of all nights to have a tour.

CUT TO
Dirt Cake percolating more and more in the landscape on shore near the Canal Boat Museum.

CUT TO
Leslie's house where a group of ladies are gathering for her Murder Mystery Winery Tour. Part of the festivities is dressing like someone from the eighties. The ladies are easily guessing who each of them is in disguise. Leslie is obviously Madonna. One lady is Tina Turner. Another is Cyndi Lauper. Molly Ringwald dressed pretty in pink is present. Carrie Fisher's Princess Leia character, Sheena Queen of the Jungle, and Linda Hamilton in her Terminator supporting role to name a few.

LESLIE. The limo bus will be here any minute. It's time to begin our Murder Mystery Winery Tour, so I need you to reach in and get your first clue before we load up.

CUT TO
Ted arriving in a twenty-six-foot U-Haul. Jay had helped rent this vehicle, as well as helped fill it with picnic tables.

Leslie, *coming out to greet him with an interrogation.* What's this? Where's the limo bus?

Ted. (*As he opens the back.*) It's broken down.

Leslie. So naturally, you get a twenty-six-foot U-Haul and fill it with picnic tables instead.

Ted. How did you know it's twenty-six feet? It's the only thing I could get on such short notice. It was Jay's idea.

Leslie. Hey, Amy! Not so fine. Ted says this was Jay's idea.

Amy. He was just trying to help. Ted was in a bind. It looks fun.

Leslie. Well, all right, load up. There might be no murderer, just victims.

Ted. I promise I'll drive real carefully.

They start to load up.

CUT TO

Series of shots *of both teams going through their warm-up drills on the football field, fans filling the stands, and the bands getting ready to perform.*

CUT TO

Jay pretending to be a photographer carefully watching the turf near the down-marker crew waiting for the game to start. He clicks away without looking through the lens.

Down-marker crew member. Excuse me, but don't you need to look through the lens?

Jay. Not if you have done this as long as I have.

CUT TO

Close shot *of a Ditchmen head and long rectangular fingers beginning to protrude from the turf near where the canister had crashed and emptied itself last night.*

CUT TO

One of the players tripping and falling flat on his face during a simple drill. The player looks around baffled, but the head and fingers quickly flatten back into the turf.

CUT TO

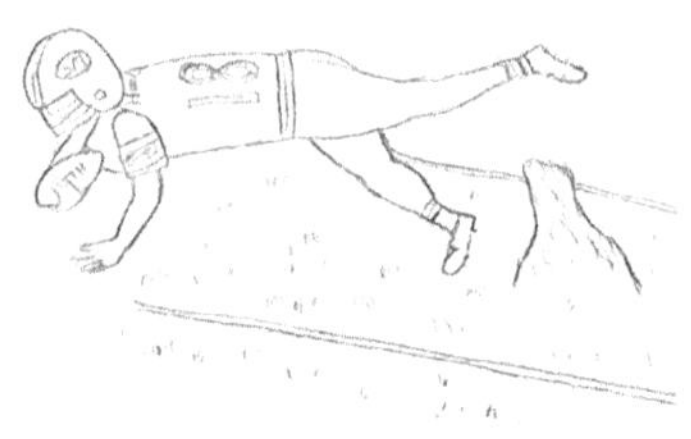

A football landing relatively near where the fingers had just emerged. A different player jogs over to retrieve it only to have the long rectangular fingers protrude again and slap the ball away from the player who also is momentarily confused and just shakes his head in disbelief.

CUT TO

Jay still staking out but doesn't see either incident.

CUT TO

The Boy Scouts' tour of the historic canal boat still in progress. The tour guide continues to spill out interesting fact after interesting fact.

CUT TO

The Dirt Cake entering the water toward the front of the canal boat. His gummy limbs start to untie the watercraft.

CUT TO

The two unhappy boy scouts whose facial expressions express their boredom.

BOY SCOUT #1. Some boat.

BOY SCOUT #2. Yea, it doesn't even move.

CUT TO
OFF SCREEN "You Got Me Rocking" by the Rolling Stones begins to play.

Dirt Cake taking off like an Olympic sprinter pulling the boat behind it right out of the canal. It heads right for the town's main street.

SERIES OF SHOTS as the song continues of Dirt Cake towing the eighty-foot-long and forty-feet-wide, at its middle, canal boat. Dirt Cake is making it move like a racing car. Also, shots of the scouts and adults hanging on for dear life.

BOY SCOUT #1 (*yelling at the top of his lungs*) This is better than a football game!

OFF SCREEN the song pauses.

CUT TO
SERIES OF SHOTS of the football pregame activities.

CUT TO
The long rectangular fingers now tripping a member of the marching band causing a domino effect to a few of the other band members.

CUT TO
Coach in the locker room beginning his pregame speech to his players.

COACH. I was reminded last night while I was grilling steaks that problems can fall right out of the sky and land right in front of you. But you got to be ready. You got to be ready for anything!

CUT TO
MEDIUM SHOT of Ted driving the U-Haul carefully down the town's main street.

CUT TO

Inside the U-Haul where Leslie and her guests have adapted to picnic tables instead of the comfortable limo bus seats. They are chatting away obviously having a good time.

CUT TO

OFF SCREEN the song continues.

Dirt Cake and the canal boat barreling down the street.

CUT TO

Ted suddenly noticing the unbelievable sight coming right toward him. He abruptly swerves just in the nick of time.

CUT TO

The ladies inside the U-Haul demonstrating some of Newton's laws of motion.

CUT TO

Dirt Cake towing the canal boat right to the high school. As it nears the fence to the football field, the Dirt Cake dissipates into the ground, and the momentum of the canal boat causes it to crash right onto the field sending Jay and the marching band running for their dear lives.

CUT TO

Coach inside the locker room wrapping up his pregame speech.

COACH. Now, let's get out there, and let us be the ones that cause surprises! Let's go, go, go!

CUT TO
Coach leading his team out of the locker room only to soon stop in their tracks.

CUT TO
The historic canal boat resting peacefully smack-dab in the middle of the field. Jay slowly walks up to it and begins helping the Cub Scouts disembark.

CUT TO
Coach surrounded by his stunned players.

PLAYER #1. Sorry, Coach. It's going to be hard to top that surprise.
COACH, *in disbelief.* You said it.

CUT TO
CLOSE-UP of the turf as a pair of dark Ditchmen-like eyes start to per-colate resembling black licorice-flavor bubble gum then disappear. Jay, due to the canal boat's grand entrance, misses this brief appearance of the Ditchmen-like eyes.

CUT TO

Ted making sure everyone in the U-Haul is all right.

LESLIE. What happened to being real careful?

TED. I had to swerve to miss the canal boat coming down the street.

LESLIE. That's your story? Canal boat coming down the street. You want to stick with that?

DISSOLVE TO

Saturday morning at the high school football stadium. Jay, Leslie, Clay, and Debbie sit quietly in the stands just staring at the canal boat being prepared to be taken off the field.

JAY. Do you guys ever stop and think just how crazy our lives have been these past two years?

CLAY. Do you ever regret always saying "enjoy the struggle"? You certainly have had to prove it these past two years.

JAY. Well, I'm surely glad I didn't say life is like a box of chocolates. I would weigh four hundred pounds by now if I had to prove that quote.

LESLIE. I feel just horrible for my thoughts last night when Ted said he swerved to miss a canal boat. I really thought he was having a mental breakdown, and there it sits, a canal boat in the middle of the football field.

DEBBIE. Which caused the game to be canceled. (*Pause.*) All of this caused by a someone who I believed in.

CLAY. He fooled a lot of people.

DEBBIE. Not you.

CLAY. Well, to be honest, my insecurity allowed me to be suspicious.

JAY. Besides Vance's Dirt Cake running loose causing havoc, Amy really believes a Ditchman is existing under that turf out there.

LESLIE. And Ted is walking into a political ambush at tonight's debate.

JAY. I sure do appreciate his courage not to separate himself from Amy but instead to embrace her work.

CLAY. We really shouldn't be worrying about all this stuff. The only thing we should be doing today is looking forward to enjoying ourselves at tonight's Ghost Ball after the debate.

JAY, *looking away into the distance.* We might have a new concern. Looks like there is one heck of a storm coming.

CUT TO

LONG SHOT of a severe thunderstorm fast approaching.

CLAY. It's coming fast. How did we not notice that coming?

JAY. We better get under the bleachers.

LESLIE, *moving down the bleachers.* I hate storms.

CUT TO

Ted and Amy arriving at the building that will be hosting the debate.

TED. This area is going to be hopping tonight. Debate right here, Ghost Ball just across the street.

CUT TO

LONG SHOT of the building hosting the Ghost Ball.

CUT TO

AMY. Oh, look, we have one protester.

TED. Just one?

CUT TO

The lone protester standing near the door. He is a young person dressed in dark clothes holding a sign that reads, "Vote for the Environment, not Scientific Progress."

PROTESTER. Wait, wait, don't go in yet. I am the only one here.

AMY. Did you really just ask us not to go in until more protesters show up?

PROTESTER. That would be the fair thing to do.

TED. The debate is a few hours away. We arrived early to rehearse. I'm sorry that you are not ready to protest us. That's your tough luck.

AMY. You need to learn to enjoy the struggle.

TED, *chuckling*. She's right.

AMY. And you need to learn the science of looking at a weather radar. There's a dandy storm about to hit.

PROTESTER. Oh, wow! Can I come inside with you?

TED. You're kidding? (*pauses*) All right, come on in.

AMY, *as they enter*. Are you being paid?

PROTESTER. Maybe.

AMY. You know that's not protesting. That's a job. There's no sacrificing on your part. A good effective protest requires some kind of sacrifice.

DISSOLVE TO

SERIES OF SHOTS of the severe thunderstorm pounding the football stadium with wind, rain, thunder, and lightning.

CUT TO

The closest and most powerful of all the lightning bolts hitting the turf field directly where the corpse and canister crash-landed two days ago. It seems to last longer than the normal lightning strike, almost like the lightning bolt that brought Frankenstein to life.

CUT TO

The foursome under the bleachers watching the lightning strike, holding their ears because of the tremendous thunder.

CUT TO

CLOSE SHOT of the turf as the storm comes to an abrupt halt.

A seven-foot Ditchman made this time out of turf slowly rises from the field leaving an impression like a gingerbread man being made by a cookie cutter from a sheet of dough.

CUT TO

The foursome slowly walking onto the field toward the Ditchman.

CUT TO

A more-slender Ditchman with no dirt on its back but instead crumb rubber, looking more like a giant gumby Bigfoot than ever before. Its front no longer grass and weeds but instead nylon or polypropylene fibers. It slowly begins to walk toward them loudly starting to sing the third verse of "'Til the Storm Passes By" in a very fast tempo.

DITCHMAN, *singing fast and loud.* When the long night has ended and the storms come no more, let me stand in thy presence on the bright peaceful shore. In that land where the tempest never comes, Lord, may I dwell with thee when the storm passes by. Till the storm passes over, till the thunder sounds no more, till the clouds roll forever from the sky, hold me fast, let me stand in the hollow of thy hand, keep me safe till the storm passes by.

CUT TO the foursome in disbelief and Jay applauding.

DITCHMAN. (*With a voice comparable to any of the legendary sports broadcasters.*) Hi, gang! Where's Amy?

JAY. Hello. Where's Amy, you ask?
CLAY. It's talking.
DEBBIE. I can't believe it.
LESLIE. Amy's with my husband, Ted, helping him prepare for his debate tonight.
JAY. You know Amy?
DITCHMAN. Of course, I know all of you. You, for example, you want a brain, you a heart. Oh, wait a minute. I'm not the Wizard of Oz. (*Laughing.*)

The foursome laughs also.

OFF SCREEN sirens are heard in the distance.

Jay. We probably need to get you out of here. There are some people who would really like to question you and I.

Ditchman. Where to then?

Jay. Duckfoot's is nearby, a real unique establishment. They wouldn't think of looking for us there. That would buy us time to make a plan.

Ditchman. Good thinking. We can duck in in there. (*More laughter follows.*) Won't we bump into some of your students? Possibly some of your classmates as well?

Jay. There, how do you know things like that?

Ditchman. I don't know. I just do. I just do.

Jay. Come on. We'll walk over. They'll recognize my truck.

Clay. Debbie and I will drive over.

Jay, Leslie, and Ditchman start walking over to Duckfoot's.

Ditchman. Say, we can do a bar rescue.

Jay. Sure, if you want to.

Leslie. I don't believe this.

Ditchman. Aw, do you need to see a counselor, Leslie? If you do, I know a good one, you! (*laughs*)

Jay also laughs, and Leslie makes a futile attempt to keep from smiling.

Ditchman. I can't drink in there. I'm underage. I'm only about ten minutes old. (*Laughs.*)

Jay. We're not going there to drink, just hiding.

OFF SCREEN *the song "Downtown" by Neil Young begins to play.*

SERIES OF SHOTS *inside the hopping bar despite it only being early evening. Duckfoot, the owner, is shown on the small stage playing his banjo. He resembles the hillbilly character from a vintage Mountain Dew or Kickapoo Joy Juice advertisement.*

CUT TO

The song's volume getting lower as Jay, Leslie, Ditchman, Clay, and Debbie enter Duckfoot's.

DITCHMAN. Jon Taffer in the house!

The rough crowd consisting of a lot of bikers oddly does not react to the new and improved Ditchman like it is no different than everyone else. Maybe they think it's a Halloween costume. Many seem happy to see Jay. He gets hugs and handshakes. He is Jay to some, Mr. Griner to others. One biker who looks a lot older reminds Jay that he was one of his former language arts students.

JAY. Wow, I can see the years have been good to you!

Ditchman seems to take the lead once inside. It walks by a group of dart players who are updating the score on a chalkboard mounted to the wall. The Ditchman reaches near the dartboard and proceeds to plug it in.

DITCHMAN. Hey, guys, it's an electric dartboard. Scores are kept automatically.

The group just looks at the Ditchman totally surprised. It then moves on stopping when it notices that the bar's floor tiles are sticking to its feet. The Ditchman lifts its leg up as Jay and Clay help pull the tiles off. The Ditchman next walks by a foosball game where it grabs a player's drink sitting on the foosball table and dumps it onto the playing field.

DITCHMAN. Rain delay!

The foosball players being tolerant, good sports break out laughing.

Ditchman then walks up onto the stage to be beside Duckfoot.

DITCHMAN, *into the mic.* Hey, Duckfoot, I'm a Ditchman even though I came from a turf. So I guess you all can call me Turfie. How about something festive? Happy Halloween! It's not a banjo song, but try and make it one.

The Ditchman begins to sing Ringo Starr's "Back Off Boogaloo."

TURFIE (DITCHMAN). (*Excerpt of the song.*) Back off, boogaloo. I said back off, boogaloo. Come on back off, boogaloo. Boo back off, boogaloo. What d'yer think you're gonna doo. I got a flash right from the start. Wake up, meathead. Don't pretend that you are dead. Get yourself up off the cart.

CUT TO
Once Turfie (Ditchman) finishes the song, the crowd goes hog wild with cheers.

DISSOLVE TO
SERIES OF SHOTS outside of the building where the debate is being held as about a hundred people now peacefully protest. Dozens of police officers guard the front door. Some of the signs the protesters hold say things like "No More Horn" and "Down with Ditchmen."

CLOSE-UP of the landscape near the front door where the mulch is extremely suspicious looking.

CUT TO
Inside the building where the debate is in progress. A group of senior citizens just finding their seats.

CUT TO
WOODY BURNS. Welcome those just arriving. As I was saying in the past three years, we have had two major Ditchmen attacks and now one attack by what is being called a Dirt Cake. The Ted Horn years are like a nightmare. What's next? Our community can't afford his friendship with Amy Griner.

The crowd gives an extremely warm applause.

CUT TO
The debate moderator, Mr. Macamee, giving Ted Horn a chance to respond. Mr. Macamee every year is the emcee of the town's summer festival, Back in the Day Days.

TED. Yes, it has been a couple of crazy years. I believe my opponent purposely mischaracterizes these incidents as attacks, especially last year when the Ditchmen were the ones being attacked. Media manipulation, plain and simple. Yes, I am good friends with Amy Griner. If she turns around and happens to find a cure for cancer or paralysis, then wouldn't all of this craziness had been worth it?

CUT TO a small applause by the audience.

AMY, *standing up*. The most recent creature is called Dirt Cake. Who here has been introducing all of us to his very own dirt-cake recipe? Vance?

Vance, *standing up*. Amy, I'm so disappointed. Choosing to blame me, the newest member to this outstanding community. Your efforts are futile, shame, shame, shame.

The crowd boos in favor of Vance Wringer.

Amy. Oh my gosh, not only do you have paid protesters. You got a paid audience too.

Mr. Macamee. Mrs. Griner, one more outburst and I'm afraid I will have to ask you to leave us this evening.

The crowd cheers.

CUT TO

Amy, *to herself as she sits down*. Most of you don't even live here. All the real citizens are at the Ghost Ball.

Amy then gets out her phone.

CUT TO

Across the street as townspeople participate in an exercise in conformity. This is because they are all basically dressed the same, covered by a sheet to resemble a ghost for their annual ball.

CUT TO

Townspeople dropping off their dogs at the Mutt Sitter dog day care. (only it's a night care tonight because of the debate and the ball)

CUT TO

Turfie the Ditchman at Duckfoot's completely surrounded by his new biker friends.

Leslie, *to Jay over all the noise*. Amy just texted me. Ted's getting raked across the coals.

Jay. We need to get over there.

Turfie. Yes, get me to this debate!

LESLIE. Amy said protesters are blocking the entrance, and the audience is mostly noncitizens.

JAY, *to anyone who can hear him.* Anybody knows a way to sneak our friend here (*meaning Turfie*) into tonight's debate. Protesters are blocking the entrance.

BIKER #1. Protesters? They just don't make protestors like they used to.

BIKER #2. He can get in my coffin.

JAY. Your coffin?

BIKER #1. His sidecar is a coffin.

BIKER #2. I use it for biker funerals and Halloween.

JAY. That's perfect. Let's go.

Jay, Leslie, Clay, Debbie, Turfie the Ditchman, and a slew of bikers pour out of Duckfoot's. They get Turfie after some extra effort into the coffin sidecar. Jay doubles up with biker #1. Clay and Debbie get into his Chevy Nova. Leslie refuses to get on a motorcycle before opting for Clay's backseat only to discover there's no floorboard.

OFF SCREEN *the song "Men Without Shame" by Phantom, Rocker & Slick begins to play at this time.*

CUT TO
Leslie in the backseat of Clay's car with no back floorboard. She starts to scream as they drive over the first of many puddles each splashing her with muddy water.

SERIES OF SHOTS *of the motorcycles racing across town as the song continues and then ends.*

CUT TO
Outside the building where the debate is taking place. It is calm before the storm. The sound of the motorcycles approaching draws the attention of both the protesters and the police officers. As the motorcycles arrive, both the protesters and the police leave their posts to greet their biker friends. It is a grand reunion.

BIKER #3, *as the hug fest continues*. What can I say, we're friends with everyone!

CUT TO

Taking advantage of this distraction, Dirt Cake emerges from the landscape and sneaks inside.

CUT TO

Jay, Clay, Debbie, and a muddy Leslie run up to the front doors, not seeing Dirt Cake, and open it up for the motorcycle with the coffin sidecar to zoom on in. This seems to break up the reunion as the protesters storm the door. Jay herds Clay, Debbie, and a muddy Leslie inside.

JAY, *to Leslie after noticing her mud-covered outfit.* Good thing you weren't already dressed for the Ghost Ball.

Jay then has a light bulb moment. Before he comes inside, he confronts the protesters with an option.

JAY. Hey, wait a minute you so-called protesters. (*Pointing to the Ghost Ball.*) Look at the Ku Klux Klan rally going on across the street!

CUT TO

Attendees of the Ghost Ball wearing sheets over their heads entering the dance.

CUT TO

The protesters who are mostly out of towners unaware that it is a Ghost Ball take Jay's bait and become enraged. They then begin a stampede across the street toward the Ghost Ball.

CUT TO

CLOSE SHOT of the farmhands sitting in a car staking out the debate site. They are confused as they watch the protesters change the location of their protest.

FARMHAND #1. Where are they going?
FARMHAND #2. They are being paid to protest a debate, not a dance.

CUT TO
Dirt Cake bypassing the auditorium entrance and continuing down a dark hallway.

CUT TO
The Ghost Ball in progress when suddenly protestors barge in and start swatting their signs at all the ghosts thinking they are members of the Ku Klux Klan.

CUT TO
The debate still in progress. Woody is wrapping up his closing statements.

WOODY BURNS. Enough of this insanity, this town needs a fresh start, and I am the fresh-start candidate!

CUT TO
Turfie, the bikers, Jay, Clay, Debbie, and a muddy Leslie walking down one of the aisles.

TURFIE, *using his booming voice.* A fresh start? What's wrong with a fantastic finish?

He continues onto the stage by himself.

TURFIE, *holding his arms up and out.* People, I am your fantastic fin-ish! (*Pauses as Ted's supporters cheer.*) Thanks to that wonderful woman right over there. (*Pointing to Amy.*) It was her desire, her sacrifices that made me, and I could lead to who knows what other discoveries.

CUT TO
A very touched Amy stands up as even more of the crowd cheers.

OFF SCREEN the roar of the Dirt Cake.

CUT TO
Dirt Cake now coming down an aisle.

CUT TO
Vance moving into the aisle ahead of the Dirt Cake to cut off Dirt Cake and make an announcement.

VANCE. No, no, this is the fantastic finish that Amy Griner and Ted Horn have plan for you. It doesn't belong here. Help me take it to where it truly belongs, with the real experts. Remember Stan Bando who was here a little over a year ago. He's the person who's got your real interest covered.

The Dirt Cake coming down the aisle stops, rears back his gummy limb, and then launches it right into Vance's gut, sending him flying way back down the row that he came out of.

The Dirt Cake then continues down the center aisle and onto the stage resembling a WrestleMania main event. He then faces off with Turfie the Ditchman.

SERIES OF SHOTS of Jay, Amy, and everyone else in the crowd filling with anticipation of the confrontation about to take place.

CUT TO
OFF SCREEN the song "Stoned Love" by the Supremes begins to play.

SERIES OF SHOTS of the confrontation across the street. Protesters are using signs to attack what they think are members of the KKK but in reality are attendees of the Ghost Ball. The ghosts fight back using the bales of straw decorations. One ghost who happens to be Coach with a whistle over his sheet and around his neck is very effective with the bales of straw. Another ghost is shown having sign after sign broke over his head with no harm to him just the signs. His sheet is eventually removed revealing that it is Stevie wearing his helmet.

OFF SCREEN *the song ends.*

CUT TO
The square off between Turfie and Dirt Cake.

CUT TO
Mr. Macamee still at his podium.

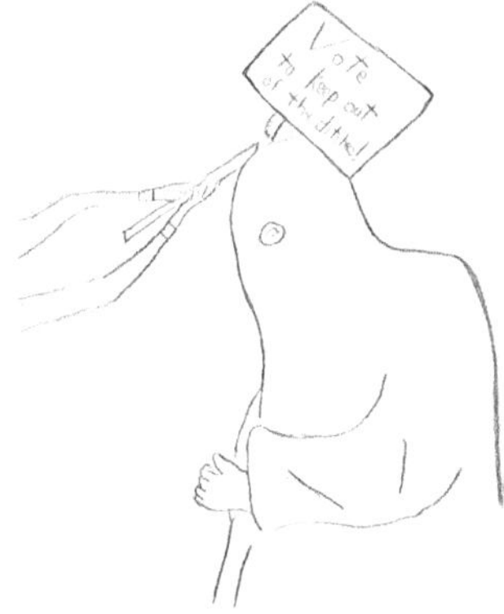

MR. MACAMEE. This is supposed to be a debate, not Big Time Wrestling!

CLOSE-UP *of him setting his timer.*

CUT TO
Dirt Cake being the aggressor and charging after Turfie who just at the right second leans back flattening his body causing the momentum of Dirt Cake to go right past the flattened Turfie. Dirt Cake roars and then comes right back again from the opposite way. Turfie repeats the same counter move, and Dirt Cake once again has its momentum go right past his target. The crowd cheers on Turfie.

Turfie then walks up to Dirt Cake doing the Mighty Igor strut, a popular legendary wrestler of the nineteen sixties and seventies. Then using its very long arms and lightning quickness, it slaps the Dirt Cake, first a couple of times on one side of its face then a couple of times on the other side. The Dirt Cake eventually gets its multiple gummy limbs up to protect the side of its face, which shouldn't be difficult since his whole body is also its face.

Turfie counters by reaching over the top of the Dirt Cake with numerous Benny Hill slap downs to it. The Dirt Cake's rage just keeps growing and is finally able to wrap up Turfie. The strongest squeeze of all time is now in full effect. It appears Turfie will be defeated. The crowd pleas for Dirt Cake to stop.

JAY. Poor Turfie. It is trapped like a doggie toy.

Nearby, Amy starts backhanding Jay in his midsection as she is struck with her own light bulb moment.

AMY. That's it! Environmental degradation. It's our only hope!
JAY. What?
AMY. We must compromise the Dirt Cake's natural environment.
JAY. We must?
AMY. It's that, or dump a bacterial biomass on it, and hope it is kryptonite to it.
JAY. How would we do that?
AMY. You would have to empty your ostomy bag on him. It's 54-percent bacterial biomass.
JAY. Uh, let's first do that environmental degradation thing. The only time I ever had my ostomy bag out in public was at the airport when they checked it for gunpowder residue.
AMY. Okay, follow my lead. (*Pause to get close.*) Turfie, get free, and follow us. I have a plan.
TURFIE. I'd be happy to!

Amy and Jay make an attempt to free Turfie. Jay grabs and pulled off a couple of the gummy limbs, while Amy took a bite out of another one. Immediately, Dirt Cake lets go of Turfie and begins to backtrack screaming in anger. The trio takes off for the exit with Dirt Cake right behind them.

SERIES OF SHOTS as a small celebration begins. Ted hugs a muddy Leslie. Clay hugs Debbie. The bikers join in too.

CUT TO
Woody and Vance disgruntled by the celebration head quickly for the exit where the farmhands are there to meet them.

FARMHAND #1. This town's crazy!
VANCE. Where did they go?
FARMHAND #2. Right out the door. We don't know how to stop these
    weird creatures around here.

CUT TO
SERIES OF SHOTS of the paid protesters losing their battle at the Ghost Ball. They are heard telling each other that this isn't a Ku Klux Klan rally as they head for the exits.

CUT TO
OFF SCREEN ACDC's "Givin' the Dog a Bone" begins to play.

Amy, Jay, and Turfie racing away from the debate venue. Dirt Cake is in pursuit but losing ground. They arrive at "Mutt Sitters."

The song pauses.

AMY. Turfie, we'll wait here. I told Jay what to do. (*Jay enters the dog
    day care establishment. He tries to pretend that he is not in a hurry.*)
EMPLOYEE. Hey, Mr. G, I didn't know we were sitting your dog.
    What's your dog's name?
JAY. Actually, I'm picking up all the dogs.

EMPLOYEE. All the dogs? How can you do that?

JAY. Well, all the owners are having such a good time at the Ghost Ball that they weren't ready to leave. I told them that I'll do them all a favor and pick up their dogs. (*Pause to look at a display of bones for sale and hands the employee his credit card.*) Here, I'd like to buy all these bones too.

EMPLOYEE. I don't think I'm allowed to release to you all the dogs.

JAY. You don't want detention, do you?

EMPLOYEE. But you're retired, and I graduated.

CUT TO

LONG SHOT of the storefront as the song resumes playing and about two-dozen dogs come running out each with a bone in their mouth. They run right past Amy and Turfie and make a beeline for the Dirt Cake. The dogs all at once make a furious effort to bury their bones into the Dirt Cake.

CUT TO

Jay, Amy, and Turfie watching from the front.

TURFIE. So that's one way to create an environmental degradation, is it?

Amy just smiles and nods.

CUT TO

Vance, Woody, and the farmhands watching from behind.

WOODY. There's not going to be anything left of it.

CUT TO
The dogs continuing to dig at the fast-dwindling Dirt Cake as they attempt to bury their bones.

CUT TO
Protesters, bruised and battered, coming from the dance toward Vance.

PROTESTERS. Hey, we deserve a bonus!

They start racing for Vance, Woody, and the farmhands who take off running for their vehicles.

CUT TO
Jay, Amy, and Turfie still watching what Amy called an environmental degradation.

AMY, *to Jay*. I'm going to need a sample of that.
JAY. Of course, you will.

They smile and put their arms around each other. INTO FRAME Turfie puts his arms around both of them.

CUT TO
AERIAL SHOT of the area as the dogs find their owners coming from the Ghost Ball.

DISSOLVE TO
OFF SCREEN the live version of the song "Let's Work Together" by Canned Heat begins to play. Months later is SUPERIMPOSED on the screen.

Turfie is busy performing its cross guard duties near a school. It is obviously enjoying his work, and the kids are enjoying Turfie.

SERIES OF SHOTS of Turfie coaching kids baseball, including how to slide into a base, which is quite easy if you are a slice of field turf and also volunteering at a nursing home pushing wheelchairs and allowing a patient to rehab their legs or hips by pretending to be the mat on a platform mounted on parallel bars. Closing credits are shown at this time. But before the credits are finished, the song ends.

CUT TO

A shelter house near Grand Lake St. Marys. A rather large family is enthralled in an enthusiastic volleyball game as part of their reunion.

CUT TO

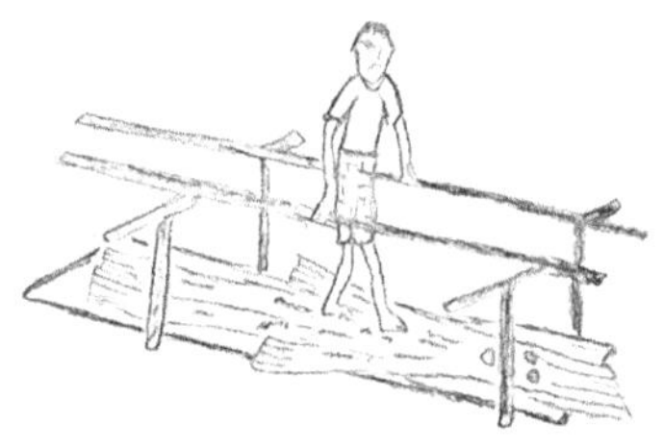

CLOSE SHOT of a red eye on the very end of a long tail possibly belonging to the legendary hodag making a snakelike maneuver toward one of the picnic tables full of food. It wraps itself around one of the legs of the picnic table and starts to pull it toward the lake. Just as it begins to enter the water, the family members take notice. They yell, and some scream as they make a futile attempt to rescue the table.

Closing credits finish being shown.

FADE OUT

About the Author

In 1984, Joe Ginter had his colon removed due to Crohn's disease along with three feet of his small intestine and his rectum. On welfare for just a month and facing the rest of his life wearing an ostomy bag and using the motto inspired by his mom, "Enjoy the struggle," he rebounded to become a fifth- and sixth-grade teacher for thirty-four years. Before his teaching career, he dabbled in stand-up comedy and writing.

With the lack of clean humor in the market, Joe decided to write *Ditchmen 1* and *Ditchmen 2* using his classes as test audiences and advisors. Ditchmen were imaginary creatures that he sketched when he was four years old as his family would drive down country roads.

Now for the 2021–2022 school year, Joe used his students, future graduates of 2029, to prepare *Ditchmen 3: The Rise of Dirt Cake* for publication. They were also very instrumental in the promoting of *Ditchmen 2: Ten Months Later*.

* 9 7 9 8 8 8 6 4 4 0 7 0 6 *